JINNSPEAK

a novella

M. S. Farzan

For Roxana
May your dreams be bigger than ours

ACKNOWLEDGEMENTS

I seem to find myself continuously indebted to the people around me for their kindness, honesty, and critique throughout my very capricious (and obsessive) writing and editing process. I am deeply grateful to my wife, Annie, and to my parents, for always being the first to read, and the last to pull punches when it comes to constructive criticism. This work in particular received quite a lot of contextual and structural polish from Waqas, Shalini, and Brian, and spectacular cover designs from Meredith.

Jinnspeak is inspired in part by the students and faculty at the Graduate Theological Union in Berkeley, CA, whose work in interreligious leadership and education continues to be foundational in my own outlook on social justice and interfaith dialogue. It is also shaped by my experience working with the good people at MMORPG.com, who know their craft better than anyone in the business.

Parts of this novella comprise my very modest attempt at paying tribute to the memory of Krishna Swaroop, whose brief presence in my life taught me more about gentleness than words can adequately express. We miss you, Uncle.

1

Zahra had never liked algebra, and she wasn't any good at it either. Although her father was an engineer—about which he took every opportunity to remind her—she hadn't inherited any of his knack for numbers.

She checked her phone for the third time in as many minutes, but her social media feed was as quiet as her little bedroom. She sighed and tossed the phone back onto her little study desk, leaning back in her chair and staring up at the ceiling for inspiration.

"If ten plus six X over three equals thirty-two, then X is..."

The plain white ceiling stared back at her, unsure.

"X is..." she repeated, feeling her patience wearing thin.

"X is stupid!" Zahra concluded, looking back down at her homework accusingly. She grabbed her phone again, bringing up an ongoing text conversation with her best friend, DJ.

What are you doing? she wrote, knowing that

he'd still be awake, and probably playing some game online.

Zahra stood up from her chair, walking over to her small dresser and peering into the attached mirror. A fat pimple marred her otherwise smooth, brown forehead, and her puffy cheeks made her look plumper than she felt. She made a face at the mirror, not liking the way she looked, and grabbed a purple scarf from the dresser. Wrapping it expertly around her wavy, chestnut hair, she pulled it slightly lower than usual to cover the pimple, and fastened it with a pink pin. It didn't match her blue long-sleeved *kameez* or jeans perfectly, but it would do.

The phone chirped, letting her know that DJ had written back to her. She adjusted her head covering once again, then walked back over to the table, looking at DJ's message.

Warlords of Gunthor, it said. *Sup?*

Zahra pursed her lips, knowing it would be hard to get him away mid-game. *I need help with math*, she wrote back truthfully, hoping she could bait him to leave his computer for an hour or so. DJ loved algebra almost as much as he loved being better at it than she was.

Ground Rules *in 15?* DJ wrote back almost instantly.

Zahra smiled to herself, texting her agreement. She tucked the phone in a pocket and looked at her textbook and notes suspiciously, not wanting to work anymore on

2

algebra tonight, or ever. She grabbed her pink backpack from the floor and dropped her homework in it unceremoniously, stuffing a light sweatshirt in over it.

She threw the bag over a shoulder and opened her bedroom door, clicking off the overhead light. Voices drifted down the hall towards her, and she smiled again. Closing the door behind her, she walked through the darkness to the well-lit living room, finding her family in their evening ritual of after-dinner TV.

"...and it's up to YOU which box to open!" A game show host's voice blared from the speaker system.

"Five!" Zahra's father shouted from his reclining chair, his white undershirt and long sweatpants letting her know he was in for the night. Her little brother, Omar, sat cross-legged at his feet in his tiny pajamas, pawing at the cream-colored carpet underneath him.

"FIVE!" Omar echoed his father, almost jumping from his seat with the effort.

Zahra's mother *tsked* from her place on the couch, folding a clean pair of boxers from a pile of laundry next to her. Her dark brown hair lay unfettered against a long plaid nightgown. "Five's *taken*, Khalid," she admonished her husband. "That was in the last round."

"*Theek hai, theek hai,*" Zahra's father said appeasingly, scanning the boxes on screen again. A young woman stood next to the game show host on TV, deliberating between a series of boxes to open as the audience yelled numbers at her.

"How about...four!" Khalid announced.

"FOUR!" Zahra's brother yelled.

"*I'm going to go with...sixteen!*" the game show contestant exclaimed at length.

"*Sixteen*," the host repeated, opening the box. "*Sixteen...is twenty dollars!*"

"Ahhhh," Zahra's father cajoled. "Should have gone with four!"

"Four!" Omar said again.

Zahra crept past the open living room towards the front door, hoping that the game show was enough to keep her family captivated and away from barraging her with questions. She had made it to the far side of the room when her mother looked up from her folding.

"Where are you going, *beta*?"

"To *Ground Rules*, mummy," Zahra said. "DJ is going to help me with my math homework."

"I can help you with your maths!" her father protested, craning his neck from around his chair.

"*Uff*, daddy," she said, exasperated. "I don't need help with chemical engineering, I need help with Algebra Two."

"It's OK, *beta*, go," her mother said placatingly. "Be back before ten."

"OK," Zahra acquiesced, tugging on her plain sneakers and opening the front door.

"I don't like them spending so much time together, Naeema," she could hear her father

4

murmur when he thought she was out of earshot.

"It's *OK*, Khalid," her mother replied. "You know they're just friends."

Zahra stepped out into the crisp night air and closed the front door behind her, hearing it latch automatically. She walked the short distance to the house's front gate, her sneakers silent against the brick path beneath. The lawn to either side of her was slick with evening dew, and a light breeze left her exposed face feeling damp. She paused, wondering if she should have brought an umbrella, then thought better of it, preferring to avoid any further interrogations from her parents.

Unlatching the waist-high gate, she left the brick path for the sidewalk, carefully closing the gate behind her. She set a brisk pace for *Ground Rules*, checking her phone to make sure she would still be on time.

Orinda's finest coffee shop was equidistant to both her and DJ's houses, and served as a popular meeting place for *Golden Mountain High School* students who wouldn't deign to be seen either at the library or the mall. It had the added benefit of being within walking distance from Zahra's parents' home, which usually forestalled any comments from them about her riding with teenage drivers who only had their permits.

The suburban streets were quiet, lit only by yellow streetlamps and hints of the moon teasing through the cloud cover. Zahra made it to *Ground Rules* in no time, the large café squatting territorially on the corner of the main thoroughfare that crossed her street. It was lively at this time of night, with several couples braving the cold, sitting outside under heat lamps and sipping at their drinks. The expansive windows were a little foggy from the indoor heating, but revealed a sizeable crowd within.

Zahra entered the coffee shop and strode up to the counter, ordering a small decaf green tea and popping a couple of sugar cubes into it. She scanned the main room for DJ and instantly spotted him, his shaggy blond hair sticking out crazily as he tinkered with his cell phone, absently sipping at an iced chocolate drink. Zahra tugged at her head covering to make sure it was still in place and walked over to his table, carefully holding her hot tea.

DJ looked up as she approached, raising his eyebrows moodily. His blue eyes were almost grey in color, and his long face with round cheeks made him look handsome and awkward at the same time. His broad swimmer's shoulders stretched at his *Magneto* sweatshirt, and his tanned skin was the only sign of his mixed heritage.

"Sup," he said noncommittally, setting his phone down on the table in front of him.

"Don't be like that," Zahra chided as she sat down across from him, shrugging off her backpack and setting down her tea. "Did I

6

interrupt an *important* fight against Gunthor himself?"

"Gunthor's not a person," her friend groused. "It's the High Council of the Archmagi."

"High Council of what?"

DJ sighed, then sipped at his drink irritably. "Never mind," he said around the straw. "Did you bring your books?"

"Yes," Zahra replied hesitantly, "but I don't want to talk about homework."

Her friend quirked an eyebrow. "But the midterm is in one month," he said slowly.

"I know, I know," Zahra said, waiting for her tea to cool. "But Winter Formal is in *two weeks*."

Understanding dawned in DJ's slate eyes. "Seriously? I skipped out on raid night to talk to you about a dance neither of us is going to?"

"Come *on*, DJ," Zahra pleaded. "You know you want to go!"

"I really don't," her friend countered, poking at his drink with the straw. "I can't dance, my…" DJ searched for the right word. "My *date* doesn't want to go, and I've got a big *Warlords* raid planned with my guild anyways."

It was Zahra's turn to be surprised. "Really? You'd rather play an online game than go to the Formal?"

DJ frowned, his thick eyebrows coming together sharply. "Don't be like that," he echoed Zahra's earlier comment, snatching his phone off the table and brandishing it at Zahra for emphasis. A screenshot of one of his game's characters stared back at her, a wizardly figure with flames for eyes and hair. "Video games are going to be my career someday, and most of my friends are from *Warlords of Gunthor*. Raid night is the only time of the week when I get to talk to all of them, and we've been planning on hitting this new dungeon for the past-"

"OK, OK," Zahra acquiesced, brushing a stray pastry crumb from in front of her. It didn't seem as if anyone had cleaned their table before DJ had sat down. "But don't you think it would be fun? It's only open to juniors and seniors, and I've never been to anything like it before."

DJ sat back in his chair, putting his phone down again and crossing his arms. "Who would you even go with?"

"Vazir," Zahra said without hesitation.

"Wow," DJ replied, impressed. "You've had *that* one locked and loaded. Did he ask you?"

Zahra shook her head, blowing on her hot tea and taking a tiny sip. "I'm thinking about asking him. I heard that he doesn't have a date, and I don't think he'd ask *me*. I think *he* thinks my parents won't let me go."

"Will they? I thought they heard about the whole underage drinking thing from last year."

Zahra shrugged, taking another sip of green tea. It warmed her belly, and sent a relaxing feeling to her fingertips. "I dunno," she said at length. "I don't think they'd be happy about it, but they wouldn't stop me."

DJ bit his fingernail reflexively, thinking.

"Will it make a difference if you go with another Paki?"

Zahra rolled her eyes at her friend. "How many times, *David Juan*," she rebuked him, using his first and middle name for effect. "Calling us 'Pakis' is like me calling you a greaser."

DJ shrugged. "Doesn't bother me," he said noncommittally. "And greaser's Italian, anyway. If you want to make fun of Mexican Americans, you have to say-"

"DJ!" Zahra interrupted him again, becoming exasperated. "Focus! Should I go to the Winter Formal with Vazir?"

"Zahra," her friend said, putting his palms out in front of him, "what do you want me to say? That I'll come with you to ask him? Or ask him for you?"

He looked at her pointedly, leaning over the table slightly. "Are you asking me to ask him for you?"

"No!" Zahra said hurriedly, sitting back in her chair and nearly spilling her tea. "No," she repeated, more quietly. "It's just, I've never asked a boy out before, and I just thought-"

"That I might?" DJ finished her sentence for her. "Because I'm gay?"

"Yes, OK?!" Zahra blurted. "Because you're a gay greaser, or whatever you want to call yourself."

DJ smirked. "I honestly think it's the only reason your parents let us hang out."

"You're not wrong."

Her friend set his drink aside, having finished it. "Zahra, you're amazing," he said seriously, warmth in his eyes. "I think anyone would be lucky to take you to the Winter Formal, and would remember it for the rest of their lives."

Zahra felt her brown cheeks flush with heat, and not from the tea. "Um, thanks?" she stammered.

"And *that's* how you ask someone out!" DJ exclaimed proudly, pumping his fist in the air.

Zahra sighed, placing her fingertips to the side of her temple. "DJ, are you going to help me, or not?"

DJ puffed himself up smugly. "I'll think about it," he said. "Now how about you make it worth my while with some algebra homework?"

Zahra scrunched up her face in irritation, but moved her tea aside and unzipped her backpack, dumping her books on the table in between them.

*****

That night, Zahra dreamed.

It wasn't one of those trances where people and places seem to be just strange enough to have the possibility of being real. Nor was it a fragmented dreamscape where each object and every character stands as a symbol for thoughts being played out in the subconscious. It was vivid, cohesive, and unlike anything she had experienced.

She was standing in a large grass field, lit only by a full, red moon overhead and frigid as a midwinter night. She shivered, but not with cold, as her body was hot, as though she had been running. Her breath turned to frost in front of her, and the only sound was the air rushing in and out of her lungs.

Zahra turned to take in her surroundings, but there was only dimly lit grass for as far as her eyes could see. She looked up at the moon, which cast the field in an eerie scarlet incandescence. Her heart beat loudly in her chest, sounding like a drum in her ears.

She turned again, and was startled to see a figure standing before her, in what had previously been an empty expanse of grass. The form was a rough outline of a human body, mirroring her own in size and stature, but wreathed completely in crimson fire. It made no motion or sound, and two almond-shaped eyes peered out at her from within the flames.

Zahra took a step backwards in her dream, afraid, but curious despite her fear. The fire spirit gave off no heat, but she felt as though her skin was hot and sweaty in the cold night. Her eyes strained to pierce the flames, but she could see nothing more pronounced than the glowing white orbs that gazed back at her.

"What," Zahra's voice was dry in her throat, falling like dry leaves onto the crimson field. "What are you?" she asked slowly of the figure standing patiently in front of her.

The fire spirit's eyes flashed once, brilliant against the flames. A voice whispered into her mind, hazy and raspy but distinguishable nonetheless.

Ana siddiquki, it spoke, the sound of crackling embers and burning twigs.

Zahra felt her brow furrow, and her courage slowly returning. "What?" she said again, taking a step forward.

The figure stood placidly, calm despite its raging form. It extended one long, flame-encrusted arm towards her, beckoning her to look at something.

She complied, following the fire spirit's arm with her eyes. The field remained red and empty, save for a shimmering, oblong portal that began to stain the horizon. The doorway rapidly moved closer, enveloping the field and blocking everything else from view. The sight of it made Zahra uncomfortable, and she could begin to see figures writhing within the flickering gateway.

Suddenly, a piercing shriek rent the air, blaring intermittently and shaking her from her reverie. The field and portal dissolved into one another, and she grasped reflexively at the fire spirit, which seemed to be frozen in mid-air. The red moon collapsed into itself, and Zahra found herself falling into a pit of nothingness.

Zahra pitched forward in her bed, breathing heavily and feeling her nightgown stick to her sweaty body. Her sleepy mind registered the sound of her cell phone's alarm, and she fumbled around her nightstand to turn it off. Exhausted, hot, and damp, she flopped back onto her pillow and stared at the ceiling, frightened.

Slowly, her breathing began to return to normal, and her wet clothes began to soothe her hot skin in the cool room. She untangled herself from the snarl of sheets and blankets and stared up at the ceiling, not wanting to close her eyes. She could still see two white, almond-shaped eyes looking back at her from a field of crimson, and hear a voice in her ears that sounded of soot and smoke.

Ana siddiquki, it said.

Zahra vowed to never drink green tea so late at night again.

2

The next day passed slowly, and Zahra felt like she was in a funk for most of the morning. Her muscles ached as though she had run a marathon, or so she presumed, as she hated running almost as much as she hated algebra. The short walk to *Golden Mountain High School* felt unending, with each step making her feel like she was moving through jello. Her mind was in a fog, alternating between ruminating about excuses for her unfinished algebra homework, and flashes of two crimson-ringed eyes floating just beyond her peripheral vision, sending her into sudden fits of sweating. Her hair felt matted under the peach-colored scarf that ringed her head, and her arms and legs felt clammy and gross beneath her green blouse and jean skirt.

First and second period were always dreary for Zahra, who never really got moving until after 10AM. After the restless night that she'd had, her first two classes were interminable. Whoever had the bright idea to schedule European Art History as the first class of the day was surely more of a morning person than

Zahra, and she spent most of the hour zoning out in the dark room, staring blankly at the projector screen. Images of Monet, Manet, Renoir, and Degas all took their place on the white wall at the front of the room, as her teacher, Mrs. Costello, droned on about Impressionist versus Realist technique. When the period bell rang and someone near the classroom door turned the lights back on, Zahra came out of her trance, realizing belatedly that she was one of the few people still sitting at a desk. Everyone except for two students speaking with Mrs. Costello — probably trying to butter her up before the midterm — had already moved on to their next classes.

The next period was better, because she shared it with DJ, and worse, because it was Algebra II, her weakest subject. They sat together at little round tables rather than at individual desks, and usually worked in partners to tackle problem sets and proofs. The fluorescent lights overhead should have been less-sleep inducing than the dark European Art History room, but Zahra still found herself struggling to pay attention to all the numbers and variables bombarding her.

"Are you even listening to me?" DJ said in his awkwardly deep voice. His blonde hair was more shaggy than usual this morning, and he was wearing a *Nine Inch Nails* t-shirt and cargo pants.

"Sorry," Zahra mumbled, trying to shake off

her tiredness. "I didn't sleep well," she offered truthfully. "What equals X again?"

"There's no X in this problem!" DJ replied, albeit a little more gently. He sighed and continued. "Y squared is equal to two Z to the power of six. So, Z must equal…"

"Miss Ahmed," a voice piped behind Zahra, "I noticed that I haven't received this week's proofs from you yet."

Zahra half-turned to see Mr. Ryan, her algebra teacher, glowering over her. He was a tiny man, only a few inches taller than her even in her seated position, with little wisps of grey hair that framed his bald brown head. His rounded spectacles made him look like a gnome, and he had cold, hard blue eyes that were softened slightly by laugh lines at the edges. His small lips were pursed in disapproval and his tiny fists were on his hips, making his baggy white button-up shirt billow out to the sides. If Zahra had been in a better mood, the scene would have appeared almost comical to her.

"I'm sorry, Mr. Ryan," she blurted, realizing she was staring at him. "Last night, I was…"

"Working on it with me," DJ chimed in smoothly, giving their teacher a winning smile. "We got through the first four problem sets, but still need to work on number five."

Mr. Ryan's gaze noticeably softened as he looked at DJ, considering his words. It was no secret that DJ was the class favorite, and that the young man's enthusiasm for math went a long way towards ingratiating him in the dour teacher's graces.

The little man harrumphed, a funny sound emanating completely from his bulbous nose, but dropped his hands from his sides in acquiescence. "Well, alright," he said begrudgingly, turning his gaze back to Zahra. "Tomorrow at the latest, then. Or you *will* lose points!"

"OK, Mr. Ryan," Zahra nodded. Her teacher harrumphed again and tottered off to another table.

"Thanks," Zahra offered to DJ weakly, managing a smile.

DJ eyed her suspiciously, the baby fat on his cheeks giving him an impish look. "Are you OK?"

"I'm fine," Zahra said quickly, feeling the blood rush to her face. The brief altercation with her teacher had been good, getting her circulation going and making her feel a bit more normal. "Now, what was X again?"

DJ sighed from the very core of his being.

*****

The next two periods were marginally better, with Zahra's Biology class providing for a stimulating discussion about cataloguing the human genome, followed by AP Spanish, which was one of her favorite subjects. As a child, Zahra had spent time with a Salvadorean babysitter, and dreamed of visiting Central America by herself when she graduated from *GMHS*. She doubted that her parents would allow it without some serious cajoling, or at least a hundred adult chaperones. A girl could dream.

When the lunch bell rang, she found herself reluctant to pack up her conjugation notebook and leave the classroom. There was something comforting about memorizing the irregular verb forms the rest of the class had been struggling with, especially with how scattered she had been feeling for most of the morning. It was nice to feel good at something.

DJ was waiting for her in the hallway, his *Nine Inch Nails* t-shirt half-tucked into his beltless cargos. He was half-turned away from her, reading a xeroxed poster pinned to one of the hallway's community bulletin boards. One of his hands stuck into his back pocket lazily, and his right knee was bent slightly, giving him the air of a male model at a photo shoot.

He'd fit right into one of the emo-rock bands he loves, Zahra thought to herself, adjusting her backpack on her shoulder. She walked over to meet him, moving in between the stream of other students rushing up and down the hallway to get to their lunch activities.

"Hey," DJ said as she approached, still reading the flier. "You see this Magic Club thing?"

Zahra looked past him at the flier, a plain

sheet of white printer paper with thick bold lettering above a clipart image of a rabbit in an overturned top hat. The text read simply:

Magic Club - Learn to Do Magic
T&Th Lunch - 5A Common Room
Email Angie at achao@gmhs.edu

The rabbit's head and paws were propped on the brim of the hat, a white-tipped black wand sticking out from under its long buck teeth. It was ludicrous.

"Magic Club?" Zahra asked, scrunching up her face at the flier. "Like, card tricks and stuff?"

DJ shrugged noncommittally. "Could be cool," he said, reaching out to grab the poster. It was loosely pinned to the bulletin board with a tack, and as he touched it, a smaller, postcard-sized flier dropped out from behind it, fluttering to the floor. DJ leaned down to pick it up, leaving the Magic Club poster in its place.

"Occult Society," he murmured, reading the postcard out loud. Zahra stood on her tiptoes to read over his shoulder. The postcard was even more simple than the Magic Club flier, just a thick piece of construction paper with black words printed in curvilinear script:

Occult Society
Mondays, 4PM Davis Library
Learn the Secret of Everything

As Zahra stared at the postcard, the script seemed to shift and squirm on the paper, sending a shiver snaking around her spine. Her face pinched again, her thin brown lips smooshing together.

"Weird," she said, poking DJ in the elbow with her finger. He seemed to be mesmerized by the postcard. "Put it back," she urged.

DJ shuddered like a wet dog shaking off water, and started sneezing uncontrollably. He slapped the flier back on the bulletin with an effort, and Zahra grabbed a stray pushpin from the board and stuck it in the middle of the postcard. She reached into her backpack and produced a napkin, which DJ accepted from her gratefully, blowing his nose.

"Lunch?" he queried, wiping his eyes.

*****

The rest of the afternoon flew by, and Zahra felt more and more like herself as the day wore on. American Literature, which was only slightly more engaging to her than European Art History, was followed by Advanced Photography, her second favorite class of the day. She spent the afternoon dissecting character development in *The Scarlet Letter* and tinkering with one of the school's sets of cameras, hoping whatever she could come up with for her midterm photo project would be good enough to make a case for a new DSLR from her parents.

PhysEd, which she didn't much care for, only met on Monday, Wednesday, and Friday, allowing Zahra to leave an hour earlier than usual twice a week. She made her way from the photo lab onto the main quad of the school, finally feeling like she was fully awake for the first time that day.

As far as Bay Area winter afternoons went, it was brilliant. The sun, although lower in the sky at this hour than it would be most of the year, still warmed the main quad, bathing it in inviting golden warmth. Green lacquered wooden benches and tables were scattered across the patio, mostly empty except for a few students reading or chatting with their friends. The quad itself was ringed on three sides by school buildings painted with the flaxen and olive hues that made up *Golden Mountain High School*'s official colors. The patio ground was an unusual mix of concrete with cobblestone, and the open side looked out on the Orinda forest, evergreens poking out over fields of tawny grass. The whole setup gave the quad a rustic, naturey look that was oddly cozy.

Zahra blinked, realizing that she was standing in the middle of the quad, staring at nothing. The sunlight felt good on her face, and she adjusted her head covering slightly, tucking a few stray brown hairs back into its folds.

She crossed the patio and reached for the heavy green double doors that led into the main building. Just as she put her hand on the metal handle, one of the doors sprung open towards her, requiring her to dash back quickly for fear of being crushed. The movement caught her off balance, and she stumbled backwards, instinctively reaching out a hand towards the rocky floor rushing towards her.

A hand caught her arm at the elbow, halting her descent. It was strong, but gentle, and kept her from hitting the floor without squeezing her too tightly. Zahra looked up from her inelegant half-standing, half-squatting position, her eyes moving up the arm to a worried, handsome brown face.

"Zahra? Are you alright?"

Zahra leaned there for what felt like an eternity, staring awkwardly at her savior. Her mind swirled with a mixture of elation and embarrassment as it took in the sight of his face, putting together the pieces of his concerned expression and weighing them against the heat that had just begun to rush to her own.

VAZIR, her mind screamed to her, annoyed. *VAZIR IS HOLDING YOUR ARM.*

Zahra realized she was staring again, and shifted her weight forward, using Vazir's grip to help her stand. For the briefest of moments, she allowed his hand to linger on her arm, her face flushed with warmth from self-consciousness and something less innocent. Prudence quickly overtook her surprise, and she gently extricated herself from his grasp. She wasn't exactly familiar with embracing men, apart from her family members and close friends like DJ, and the sensation made her a little uncomfortable.

"Sorry," she offered meekly, readjusting her backpack on her shoulders.

"No, I'm sorry," Vazir replied, concern still showing on his face. His black eyebrows were furrowed together over his hawkish nose, and his boyish frown marred an otherwise handsome visage. His eyes were a luxurious mahogany, with flecks of darker brown that made his irises look like tree trunks. Jet black hair was swept casually to one side of his head, and tapered neatly around his caramel-colored ears.

"It's OK," she said, managing a little smile. Her heart was beating and her mouth felt dry, and not just from the near fall.

HE SMELLS NICE, her mind yelled at her.

At long last, Vazir grinned back at her, and it lit up Zahra's afternoon at least as much as the sunshine. White teeth appeared teasingly between his full lips, and his brow unfurrowed to reveal smooth, unblemished brown skin. He was a year older than her, in his senior year, and the age difference showed. He looked more a man than a boy, or to Zahra's eyes, a fashion model.

"Good," he said charmingly. His voice lilted slightly at the end of each word, his accent almost unnoticeable except to Zahra, who had been hearing Urdu all of her life. Even to her ears, his inflection sounded a little exotic, adding to his allure all the more. "Where are you going?"

"Um, home," she said simply, unsure of how to hold a conversation with him. For all of the time that she spent thinking—and with DJ, talking—about him, she had only spoken with Vazir a handful of times. Their families knew each other from a shared religious community, and she often saw him at cultural events or with mutual friends around school. Now faced with an opportunity to engage with him one-on-one, she realized she was completely out of her depth.

Fortunately, Vazir was willing to pick up the slack. "Oh, can I give you a ride? I'm going home, too."

Zahra's heart skipped a beat. Alone? With Vazir? In his *car*? She wasn't sure if the look on DJ's face when she told him the story would be worth the amount of trouble she would be in when her parents found out.

For the second time that afternoon, prudence won out. "Ah, no thank you, Vazir," she said politely, relishing the opportunity to have his name on her lips. "It's just a few blocks from here, I can walk."

Vazir's smile held. "No problem," he said, unfazed. He was persistent. "Say, are you going to the Winter Formal?"

Zahra's mind screamed at her again, unintelligibly this time. She felt herself freeze, excited and scared at the same time.

"No," she said quickly. "I mean, not yet," she immediately corrected herself. "I mean, I don't have a date yet."

"Oh," Vazir responded smoothly. His smile widened, and he put his hand out towards her, almost like an invitation. "Do you want to go together? I don't have a date either."

A million questions jumped to Zahra's screeching mind, not the least of which being her incorrect assumption that he wouldn't initiate conversation with her about the Winter Formal.

Does he actually like you that much? Her mind asked her curiously. *Is he really asking you to go to Winter Formal with him? What will your parents say when they find out that you want to go, and with a boy?*

None of the questions mattered, she realized quickly.

SAY SOMETHING, she could hear her mind's prompting as though it was blaring through the quad's PA system.

"I do," she blurted, realizing belatedly that she was agreeing to go to a high school dance, not to get married.

"Great!" Vazir said, his eyes lighting up to match her own excitement. "I'll text you this weekend?"

"Yes, sure," Zahra said dazedly, fumbling in her skirt pocket for her phone. They exchanged phone numbers, and Vazir smiled at her again before continuing on his way to the student parking lot, promising to be in touch.

If Zahra knew how to skip, she would have capered all the way home.

*****

Zahra's dream that night was ten times more intense than the previous one.

Whereas her awareness in the first dream was limited to sight and sound, this time, the rest of her senses came alive. Her skin, although a more normal temperature now, felt the coolness of a strong breeze caressing her body, whipping her nightgown around crazily. She remained standing on an open field, and could smell the earthiness of the grass, along with the tang of brimstone and, ever so faintly, something more sinister. The taste of smoke played across her tongue, not unlike the sensation she had once experienced when an uncle had found it amusing to share a hookah pipe with his children and their cousins at a family party.

The field was as desolate as it had been in the first dream, bathed in scarlet light by the red moon. Almost anticipating the next part of the vision, Zahra turned, finding as expected the fire spirit waiting for her.

It looked the slightest amount more human, its fiery body contained within an anthropomorphized outline. Four limbs extended from a cylindrical torso, topped by a vaguely oval head. The two almond-shaped slits

26

serving as eyes bored into her soul, but seemed infinitesimally less menacing to Zahra's sleepy brain than they had a night before. Flames licked up and down the figure, filling Zahra's nostrils with the smell of burning coals, and touching her gently with their warmth.

Ana siddiquki, the voice rasped into her mind.

The analytical portion of Zahra's brain began to stir, and she slowly understood that the figure meant her no harm - the opposite, in fact. She nodded, not quite comprehending, but willing to pay attention.

Ana siddiquki, the figure repeated, again extending one of its arms to point behind her.

Zahra turned, and the portal was there, widening and expanding to drown out the grassy field and the horizon beyond it. Dark figures roiled within, tearing at each other and everything around them, whispering and snarling, a frightening susurrus on the frigid wind.

As with the first dream, a peal rent the night air, causing the portal to collapse on itself, greedily enveloping the field, the fire spirit, and the red moon with it. Zahra grasped at nothing, falling into the portal, the clarion reverberating in her ears and thrusting her into consciousness like a swimmer cresting the surface of a turbid stream.

She sat up in bed, sweating, her wet hair plastered to her forehead. She breathed as though for the first time in a long while, sucking in her room's stale air and feeling her lungs expand and her body return to normal. Like the previous night, she could still see the fire spirit's white eyes and hear its hoarse voice on the wind, but her vision was taken up almost completely by the image of the portal, its roiling depths swallowing everything in its path.

In contrast to the night before, she was no longer fearful of the fire spirit, which seemed to want to help her. She still knew no more about what it was saying or what it wanted, but she intuited that it wouldn't hurt her.

The portal, on the other hand, was unquestionably a thing of evil. She couldn't place a finger on it, but she knew her fear from the night before had nothing to do with the fire spirit, her only ally in the murky darkness of the portal on the crimson field.

Tonight, she was afraid for another reason entirely.

3

It had been a week, and Zahra's dreams had shown no sign of letting up. Each night, she dreamed of the fiery figure on the ruby plain, tumbling through the frightening portal into consciousness with the words *ana siddiquki* ringing in her ears. Each morning, she begrudgingly rustled herself out of her sweat-drenched sheets, padding barefoot into the little bathroom that she shared with her brother. She began her day with her morning ablutions, first washing her hands and swishing water around her mouth three times. She cupped water in her right hand, lifting it to her nose and quickly inhaling and expelling it through her nostrils, cleaning her nose. She then splashed her face three times, grateful for the cool water that did much towards calming the lingering heat from her dreams. She washed her arms up to her elbows, wiping her head, ears, and neck, and stuck her feet one at a time in the sink, cleaning in between each of her toes.

Every morning, Zahra continued her ritual by returning to her room, wrapping a simple silk scarf around her head, and performing her prayers. Unlike a lot of Muslims, who endeavored to pray five times a day at prescribed times, Zahra only prayed when she could, finding it extremely difficult — even embarrassing — to make the space at school. She would have to find an empty room and excuse herself from one or more of her classes to do so, and was loath to draw any more attention to her faith. She was already uncomfortable being one of the handful of *hijabi* girls at *GMHS*, and didn't like the thought of having to explain why she was allowed to leave American Literature or Algebra II to pray in a closet somewhere on campus.

Her mornings at home, however, were her own. Zahra's parents, more religiously observant than she was, but not very strict with details, would encourage her to pray as often as she could, and to join them in visiting their local *masjid* for big holidays and special gatherings. She couldn't motivate herself to wake up before sunrise, the time at which the first invocation of the day was traditionally performed, but she nonetheless made it a point to begin her day with prayer.

Zahra pulled a small rectangular rug out from a cubby under her desk, spreading it across an open space on her carpeted floor. The rug was a gift from her grandfather when he visited from her extended family's home in Islamabad, a souvenir he had picked up when he performed the *hajj* pilgrimage to the city of Mecca. It was a brilliant blue and red color, with yellow accents, and depicted the holy site of the *Ka'aba*, a cubic house thought of as the heart of Mecca and said to be built by the prophet Abraham. The carpet was soft to the touch and had blue tassels that were almost neon in color. She angled it in a northeasterly direction, known to be the shortest route to the *Ka'aba*, and began her prayer by crossing her hands upon her chest, reciting the first chapter of the *Qur'an* in Arabic.

"*Allahu akbar*," Zahra spoke quietly into the morning, feeling her senses coming to life, if sluggishly. She bent down once, continuing to recite, then stood up straight, keeping her eyes fixated at the front of the rug beneath her.

"*Allahu akbar*," she continued, gently placing her knees on the carpet, then her hands, then her forehead. She repeated a litany of prayers in Arabic, sitting up straight once, then prostrating herself again. Then she stood once more, and repeated the cycle.

At the end of the prayer, she sat with her feet folded beneath her and palms outstretched in front of her, speaking ritual words of supplication that she had memorized from her parents and different religious functions at the *masjid*. She knew very little Arabic outside of her prayers, and wouldn't even be able to order a coffee if she found herself in an Arabic-speaking country, but she at least understood the English meaning behind her prayers.

Her ritual complete, Zahra tossed on some

clothes, exchanging her head scarf for something more formal, and rushed down the hallway to the kitchen, stuffing books into her backpack as she went. Her family was usually up before her, bustling about the kitchen or eating breakfast.

This morning, her father was sitting at the round wooden table in the center of the room, his feet crossed under the table and the morning newspaper spread out in front of him. Her brother sat across from him, happily shoveling marshmallow cereal into his mouth with a Mickey Mouse-shaped spoon. Zahra's mother stood at the kitchen's long counter, carefully swathing sandwich halves with plastic wrap.

"Good morning, *beta*," her mother chirped as Zahra entered the room, hearing her approach. "Did you sleep well?"

"*Uff*, mummy," Zahra groused, grabbing a piece of toast from the table. "Not at all."

"Oh, I'm sorry *beta*," her mom said kindly, turning from her work and wiping her hands. "Did you drink that green tea again?"

"No," Zahra said morosely, looking at her brother. He grinned, green and purple marshmallows staining his teeth.

"I'm sorry," her mother repeated, the tiniest bit of reproach in her voice. "Hopefully you can get to bed *earlier* tonight."

"Yes, mummy," Zahra replied perfunctorily. She pulled a piece of crust off the toast and popped it in her mouth. On a whim, she decided to bring up a topic that had been on her mind since the previous week.

"Can you take me to the mall after school? I need some new clothes."

"New clothes? You just got some new outfits for *'Eid*," her mother replied, turning to place the sandwiches into individual lunch bags.

"I know," Zahra said slowly, debating. She wasn't comfortable with where the conversation might lead, but decided to press her luck. "I need a dress for the Winter Formal next week."

The kitchen got very quiet, the silence disturbed only by the sound of her brother's spoon scraping the bottom of his cereal bowl. Zahra saw her mother stiffen slightly, but continue to stuff lunch bags.

"What about the Winter Formal, *beta*?" her mother said carefully, without turning around.

"I just," Zahra stammered, realizing belatedly that this likely wasn't the best time to bring up such a sensitive topic. "Vazir asked me to go to the Winter Formal with him," she blurted, feeling the words pour out of her like a leaky faucet, "and I need something nice to wear."

For the first time since Zahra had entered the kitchen, her father looked up from his newspaper, eyeing her over his round glasses. His thin, white eyebrows drew together, standing out in stark contrast against his brown skin.

"What is this Winter Formal?" he queried.

"It's a school event," Zahra's mother said quickly, half-turning from the counter. Ever the mollifier, she would often use choice words to play down the significance of social situations, knowing which topics could potentially ignite a family argument. Zahra knew her mother was avoiding using the terms "co-ed" or "dance," either of which would be taboo to her father's very conservative tendencies.

"Next Thursday," Zahra said. "All of my friends are going, and there will be teacher chaperones," she added quickly.

Her father's expression didn't change. "What kind of event is it?"

"It's like, a group thing," Zahra stuttered, finding it difficult to tiptoe around the subject. "My friends will be there, and there will be a D.J.…."

Zahra's voice trailed off as her father's eyebrows came together even more sharply, if such a thing were possible. She knew her father well enough to tell when he was angry, or at least uncomfortable. In her family, it was rare for unmarried members of the opposite sex to spend time together outside of certain religious functions or at least under the supervision of close family members. Her parents tolerated her friendships with DJ and a handful of other male friends, but going to an event with a potential suitor like Vazir was of another league entirely. That such an event would be a dance, with underage students in all manners of dress, gyrating to unabashedly sexualized pop music, made the proposition of Zahra's attendance all the more questionable.

"Boys and girls?" Zahra's father asked. It was more of a statement than a question.

She nodded.

Zahra's father stared at her for another moment, and the silence hung between them, stifling in the small room. Even Zahra's brother stopped eating his cereal, and looked back at their mother, whose expression was unreadable.

Without saying a word, her father turned back to his newspaper. Zahra felt a door shut between them, and was unsure as to how she should proceed.

Her mother broke the silence first. "Let's talk about this later, *beta*," she said, gliding across the kitchen floor and handing her a lunch bag. "Have a good day at school."

Zahra nodded mutely, wiping forgotten bread crumbs from her hands. She took the lunch bag and walked out of the kitchen quietly, grateful to exit the suddenly tension-filled room.

Her father continued to stare at his newspaper, not looking up as she left.

*****

As had been the case for the past week, Zahra's mind and body didn't seem to get going until around lunchtime. She dozed through most of European Art History, and only managed to stay awake through Algebra II by virtue of DJ's constant elbowing. Biology and

AP Spanish were marginally better, but more often than not Zahra found herself staring out *GMHS'* horizontal windows, looking at but not seeing the evergreen trees just outside, and listening to but not hearing her instructors. Her mind alternated between excitement and trepidation about going with Vazir to the Winter Formal, which inevitably led to uncertainty because of the morning conversation with her parents. Lurking behind every thought, just beyond her conscious daydreaming, was a dark, gaping portal, waiting patiently for her to complete her day and fall asleep.

As was his habit, DJ was waiting for Zahra in the school hallway after her AP Spanish class. His moody expression was more dour than it had been during Algebra II, and his grey *Misfits* t-shirt looked out of place in contrast with his designer jeans. The faded skull on his t-shirt grinned slyly at her as she approached.

"What's the matter?" she asked.

DJ shrugged, shaking his floppy blonde hair out of his face. "Nothing," he said, turning to walk briskly towards the school cafeteria.

Zahra hurried after him, concerned. "What do you mean, 'nothing?'"

"I don't want to talk about it," DJ said, making his way through the flow of students moving up and down the long hallway.

Zahra stepped over the outstretched legs of a student who was sitting with her back against the hallway wall. She grabbed DJ by the elbow, who turned back towards her crossly.

"What?" he fumed.

"David Juan," she chided, feeling heat rise to her face. "I think I'm getting disowned for going to the Winter Formal next week, and I haven't been sleeping well. If there's something going on, please just tell me. I don't have the patience for much else right now."

DJ's visage softened somewhat at Zahra's comment. He shuffled awkwardly, putting his thumbs underneath the straps of his backpack. "I asked Jason to the Formal, and he said no."

"Oh, I'm sorry," Zahra said, grateful that she was already holding his arm. She silently berated herself for being so focused on her own problems that she hadn't given much thought to her friend's plans. "You asked him after Algebra?"

DJ nodded, looking into an open classroom across the hallway from where they stood. A group of students were inside, tinkering with a large, colorfully painted wooden box propped on top of a desk.

"What did he say?" Zahra prodded gently.

Her friend shrugged again, looking back at her. There was a shadow of pain in his blue eyes. "Something about not being ready for the world to know about us, or some B.S."

Zahra nodded, understanding. DJ and Jason had an on-again, off-again relationship, mostly because of the latter's insecurity around others about his sexual orientation. DJ had come out to

Zahra and a small number of other mutual friends only a year ago, but from what Zahra knew about Jason from DJ—which was admittedly very little—he wasn't quite ready to share something so private with anyone.

"I'm really sorry," Zahra said again, squeezing DJ's arm.

"Thanks," DJ said, smiling slightly and shrugging for a third time. "What's this about you not sleeping?"

A loud *BOOM* issued from the room across from them, and both Zahra and DJ turned instinctively towards the sound. The students within stood a couple feet away from the desk, which was placed directly in view from the hallway. They gawked at the colorful box, which had a tiny puff of smoke emanating from its top.

"*Double-U tee eff,*" DJ said to no one in particular, weaving through the students that had stopped in the hallway to see what the commotion was about.

Zahra followed DJ, not as graceful as he was moving through the crowd, but still able to push her way to the open doorway. A small placard above the door read "*5A - Common Room,*" and she recalled that this classroom was ordinarily used by special interest groups, like *Say Yes,* the school's improv troupe, and *GMHS*'s chapter of *Model United Nations.* Zahra vaguely remembered the flier DJ had picked up last week for the Magic Club, which would be meeting today.

The room opened up to the right of the doorway, with single-person desks lined neatly in rows and columns of six. They were for the most part empty, except for two desks near the head of the classroom, which had a student apiece standing precariously on top of them, looking over the shoulders of the little group engaged with the colored box.

The box, Zahra noticed as she entered the room, was more of a long wooden crate, placed awkwardly on the teacher's table beneath. It was painted in fantastically slapdash pastel colors, pink and mauve clashing fabulously against canary and baby blue. The palette had no discernable pattern, save its gaudiness, and the type of wood beneath was inscrutable under what looked like several coats of paint.

Two students stood in front of the crate. One of them still gaped at the box, balancing expertly on a pair of forearm crutches and seemingly mesmerized by the puff of smoke that was rapidly dissipating in the room's warm air. The other was helping a third student clamber his way out of the crate's top, holding him under the arms and helping him to scoop himself through an open panel that was hinged to the side of the box.

"Nothing! *Nothing!*" the student blustered as he slithered clumsily through the panel, waving towards the open doorway behind Zahra and DJ. A small throng had gathered just outside, curious about the commotion. "I'm OK! Everything's *OK!*"

Zahra and DJ exchanged a quizzical glance.

"Everything's OK," the student repeated, finally extricating himself from the panel and waving away his compatriots. He remained standing on the table, his feet and ankles still swallowed by the crate, and his pale, long legs peeked out from under black slacks that were rolled up to just below his knees. He was beanstalk-thin, and an oversized tuxedo jacket with coat tails sagged around his wiry frame. His angular face was red with exertion, or embarrassment, and his close-cropped blonde hair was almost white in color.

Satisfied that they had either missed the action, or that whatever had occurred wasn't all that interesting, the hallway crowd began to disperse. One of the students by the desk, a Chinese American girl with a pretty apricot blouse and blue jeans, stared up at the tuxedoed boy and *tsked*.

"It doesn't *work*, Theo," she protested. An orange bow matching her blouse tied her black hair together festively. "If you pull the lever before unhinging the panel, you don't have enough time to escape before the smoke clears."

"I'm telling you, Angie, it works!" Theo countered, his voice cracking. He bunched his abnormally long hands into fists. "I got it to work last night at home!"

"*Mmm hmm,*" Angie folded her arms across

her chest, unconvinced.

One of the pair of students standing on the single-person desks chimed in. "Remind me why you can't change the timer on the smoke machine, again?" Zahra recognized him as Tayo, one of the school's exchange students from Nigeria. His twin sister, Tamba, stood next to him, and they wore charmingly matching outfits of tan khakis and dark blue polo shirts. Tayo wore a green and gold *GMHS* Soccer Team cap, while Tamba's curly, auburn-dyed hair lay unfettered against her shoulders.

"Ugh, the smoke machine is *connected* to the lever," Tamba chided her brother. "The lever overrides the timer."

"Just unhinge the panel first then," Tayo said reasonably.

"It's not that simple!" Theo groused.

"I thought it was just...*amazing*," the student standing next to Angie said breathlessly. Zahra didn't know her name, but recognized her from the slate-colored forearm braces. She had a kind, chubby freckled face and fiery red hair that was pulled back into a high ponytail. A yellow flannel shirt peeked out from under her denim coverall dress, and her skinny, stockinged legs tapered into oversized black orthopedic shoes.

"It'll be amazing when it *works*, Bridget," Angie countered. Bridget stuck her tongue out in response.

"*Ah-herm*," DJ cleared his throat audibly. "What...what are you all doing?"

As one, the little group turned towards DJ and Zahra, seemingly self-conscious that their private squabble had been observed by outsiders. To his credit, Theo recovered the most quickly, puffing up his chest and sweeping his lanky arms out to either side.

"Magic," he said dramatically, his voice cracking.

Angie rolled her eyes. "Theo's trying to do this disappearing wizard illusion we've been working on," she explained, speaking to DJ, "but he's having trouble sticking the landing."

"I *told* you," Theo complained, "It worked last night, but the smoke machine…"

"I'm Angie," Angie said, ignoring her compatriot and striding across the room. She extended a hand, which DJ took, and named each of the group in turn. "That's Tamba, her brother Tayo, Bridget, and you've seen Theo."

"DJ," DJ said for himself simply.

"I'm Zahra," Zahra said, shaking Angie's hand and giving the others a friendly wave.

"So do you all do, like, sleight of hand stuff?" DJ asked, genuinely intrigued. Zahra knew he loved every type of magic, particularly the sword-and-sorcery kind that one could find in role-playing video games.

"Bridget's our card and coin expert," Angie said, nodding towards the girl on crutches behind her. "Tayo and Tamba do mirrors, and Theo's our vanishing trick person."

"*Illusionist*," Theo corrected.

"Whatever," Angie said.

"What do you do?" Zahra asked.

"Mind reading," the girl replied, her eyes flashing. "But mostly just keeping everyone here in step."

"That's cool," DJ said, nodding his head excitedly. "I've been trying to do a false cut but can't even seem to fool my little sister."

"What kind of false cut?" Bridget asked from behind Angie. She swiveled one of her crutches around and leaned on it casually. "One-two cut? Up the Ladder?"

"Um," DJ stuttered.

Bridget waved the hand that she wasn't using for balance. "Nevermind. I can show it to you."

"Are you all interested in magic?" Tamba asked, climbing down from her perch to stand next to her brother, who had sat down on the front of his desk.

"He is," Zahra said, pointing at DJ. "He plays a wizard in *Warlords of Gunthor*."

"Blood Sorcerer, actually," DJ said.

"What server are you on?" Theo asked from atop the teacher's desk.

"U.S. Pacific," DJ replied. Zahra could see something change in her friend's posture, as though he were looking at the skinny student in a new light.

"Nice, me too," Theo said, putting his hands in his tuxedo pockets. He seemed to have forgotten that he was still standing in the colorful box. "Water Shaman."

"Nice," DJ echoed enthusiastically. "Got a raid group? My guild's looking for more."

"I'll add you!"

"*Anyway*," Angie said, clearly having heard enough. She pointedly looked at her watch, and back at Zahra and DJ. "The class bell is about to ring, but we meet up every Tuesday and Thursday if you want to join us."

"I'm down," DJ said.

"Um, sure," Zahra said uncertainly. She didn't have DJ's zeal for magic, but something inside of her urged her to agree. On a whim, she voiced what was on her mind.

"Do you all know anything about...portals?" she asked, almost sheepishly.

"Like, *Doctor Who*?" Tayo asked, rising from his seat. The class bell rang as he did so, indicating that the students had five minutes to get to their next classes.

Zahra didn't understand the reference. "Doctor what?"

"No, *Who*," Tayo said.

"What?"

"It's not important," Tamba cut in. "What kind of portals? Teleportation?"

"No," Zahra replied, unsure. "Like, *dark* portals. With monsters in them, or shadows, or something."

The twins looked at each other, and back at Zahra. They shook their heads simultaneously.

"That sounds like something from *Warlords*," Theo piped in, finally clambering out of the crate and off of the desk.

"It does," DJ agreed thoughtfully, looking at Zahra with a question in his blue-gray eyes. "What are you saying, Zahra?"

"I...I don't know," she said honestly. "Sorry, I was just wondering. I don't know anything about them, I just thought..."

"You might try the Occult Society," Angie offered, sliding an orange knapsack that almost matched her blouse over one shoulder. "That kind of thing is their specialty. But they're..." She seemed to be searching for an accurate descriptor.

"Weird." Bridget finished Angie's sentence for her, expertly using her crutches to help her move towards the classroom door. Tamba and Tayo hastened to join her.

"OK," Zahra said dubiously. "I'll try them." She looked at DJ, who shrugged.

"Alright, well, come by next time if you want?" Angie repeated her invitation as she made her way to the hallway. DJ and Zahra murmured their agreement, following her out to find their next classes.

"Hey!" Theo's voice squeaked querulously from the room behind them. "Is anyone going to help me put this thing away?"

4

The Winter Formal approached more quickly than Zahra had thought possible. Her classes and homework had begun to focus in earnest on the upcoming midterms, and she had had little time for anything besides school and studying. Almost every evening, she would meet DJ at *Ground Rules* to work on algebra and chat about the Winter Formal, joining a handful of other students who preferred to study in the bustling coffee shop rather than at the library or at home.

Any trepidation about attending the Winter Formal was far outweighed by Zahra's excitement to have something outside of her normal schedule to look forward to. She was ordinarily a good student—except when it came to algebra—but the lack of restful sleep had begun to affect her concentration, even in the afternoons and evenings. She felt like a zombie, treading ponderously through a dreamscape, occupying a facsimile version of herself that was slower, heavier, and not as smart as her former self. She went through the motions of attending her classes, responding to questions perfunctorily, and only regaining some semblance of mental quietude during her morning prayers and in the small hours of the night before she went to bed. The rest of her days were occupied with thoughts of shadows darting in and out of her conscious mind, greedily devouring her energy and her will to resist them, while crimson-rimmed orbs stared back at her from the pages of her textbooks.

Meeting with the Magic Club again had drawn Zahra out of her shell a bit. On the Tuesday after she and DJ had met them for the first time, the group worked on a mirror-based illusion with Tayo and Tamba, where the twins switched places in a makeshift cabinet, performing in front of an imagined audience of their peers. The Thursday of the Winter Formal, they met again at lunch, and Bridget showed DJ some card tricks as she had promised the previous week. He seemed to have a knack for sleight-of-hand, and was a quick study. They were a cheery team, and it warmed Zahra's heart to hear that they would be attending the Winter Formal together that evening. Their enthusiasm for the event convinced DJ to forgo his guild's raid night and join them instead, and Zahra hoped that their friendly faces might help quell her own nerves.

With some reticence, her mother had helped her shop for a new outfit for the event, driving her all the way to Berkeley to check several different South Asian boutiques for formal wear. Zahra knew that she didn't want to wear something too formal, but didn't feel comfortable wearing anything too Western, either, which eliminated quite a few types of clothing. Dresses were out, and while she liked the idea of wearing a *saree* that covered her shoulders and midsection, the ones that she tried on made her look like she was a heroine from one of the Bollywood films that her mother loved so much. Although both of her parents were from Islamabad, her mother had spent some of her childhood years in India, where Zahra's grandfather had worked for a time. Zahra's parents still watched some of the older, tamer Bollywood classics now and then, and their vivacious costumes and catchy soundtracks had made a strong impression on the Pakistani girl as a child.

In the end, Zahra had decided to go with a modest, mint-colored *kameez* with a matching *shalwar*, and a beautifully embroidered shawl that would serve as her *hijab*. They were each made from a combination of velvety polyester fabric under a sheen of faux chiffon, soft to the touch but not overly warm. The *kameez* covered her torso, arms, and bottom, while the *shalwar* draped baggily along her legs and covered her ankles. She matched a pair of shiny eggshell flats to complement her attire, and used a simple fake ivory needle to pin her hijab together, only allowing her hands and her face to be visible.

She checked her appearance for the hundredth time in the mirror on her room's dresser. She thought she looked okay, by her own standards, but was well out of her depth when it came to fashion, and had never been comfortable with her overweight body type. The pimple on her face had finally relented, but her ordinarily smooth, nut-brown skin looked pale to her from lack of rest. Two uninspired brown eyes looked back at her from within the mirror, contemplating her appearance. Zahra couldn't shake the impression that they were ringed in fire.

She realized that she was stalling, not just because she was nervous about attending the Winter Formal with a boy, but also because she dreaded the conversation she was bound to have with her parents on her way out the door. Her mother had barraged her with advice and questions on their shopping spree, wanting to know who would be at the dance, who were the chaperones, when she would be home, and whether Vazir's parents knew that the two teenagers were going together. Zahra had answered the questions as best as she could, and listened respectfully as her mother forewarned her about alcohol-spiked punch at teenage parties and how Western pop music was un-Islamic. She tried not to roll her eyes at her mother's conservative outlook on almost everything related to the Winter Formal, but it was a challenge.

Her father hadn't spoken to Zahra since their brief discussion the previous week. She knew that she had crossed some sort of line in wanting to go to the dance with Vazir, but didn't always understand her parents' reactions to social situations that seemed commonplace to her non-Pakistani friends. When her parents were cross with her, they would give her the silent treatment, which she hated, but she couldn't grasp why her father would be mad at her for wanting to attend the Winter Formal. She could only surmise that it had something to do with not respecting tradition or her parents' wishes, but it was hard to understand his mood when he wouldn't speak to her.

Zahra took a deep breath, adjusting the pin on her *hijab* nervously, and left her little room, quietly closing the door behind her. She padded down the hallway, hearing only the sound of television voices from a show the rest of her family was watching in the living room. She came to the opening of the room trepidatiously, smoothing the front of her *kameez* with her hands. She was sure at least her mother would make a complimentary comment about her outfit, and was uncertain as to what her father would have to say.

Her family had claimed their usual TV-watching perches, and her mother sat on the couch, working a needle and thread through one of her father's white undershirts. Her brother, Omar, was lying on his stomach, playing quietly with a pair of metal-wrought painted toy cars. Zahra's father reclined in his cushioned chair, watching what looked like an environmental documentary.

Her mother glanced up as she entered, a look of guarded indifference across her face. She paused in her sewing, and Zahra braced for whatever conversation might ensue.

"Don't be late, *beta*," her mother said simply, and went back to work on the undershirt. Her father kept his eyes on the documentary, and said nothing.

"Um...okay," Zahra said. Bemused, she turned away from the room and squared her shoulders, trying not to feel deflated from the anti-climactic exchange. She grabbed a heavy jacket from near the house's entryway and opened the front door soundlessly, escaping into the night.

*****

Golden Mountain High School was a college preparatory school of some affluence, and the administration spared no expense when it came to events. The entire basketball gymnasium had been repurposed for the Winter Formal, decorated in frosty themes for a season that rarely touched the temperate Bay Area. Icy blue and green streamers framed every doorway and dangled at intervals throughout the gym, bringing to mind swirling breezes and polar lights from distant regions. Plastic snowflakes and papier-mâché mountains were taped to the gigantic room's white walls, and a trail of blue-and-white Christmas lights ringed the entire gymnasium, complementing the dim ambience with their twinkling warmth.

A long row of tables was set up neatly against one side of the gymnasium, packed to the edges with winter-themed drinks and treats. There were huge bowls of blue punch interspersed among packets of gummy polar bears and soda cans that had been individually wrapped in tiny red-and-white scarves. Steaming thermoses filled with hot chocolate stood next to platters of brownies, sugar cookies, and white chocolate snowballs, and each table was ringed with shimmering silver tinsel that had the appearance of icicles in the dim light. On the opposite side of the room, the normally ubiquitous metal bleachers had been cunningly hidden inside the gymnasium wall thanks to a considerable amount of engineering foresight on the part of the gym's architect, and the basketball hoops were pulled back to rest against the lofty ceiling.

The lacquered wood floor was the only surface in the gymnasium that was left untouched, and provided for a natural, if enormous, dance area. A D.J. booth at the very far end of the room produced loud, blaring pop music from a series of upright speakers spread throughout the gym, and provided a meager source of color through rotating LED stage lights. The thumping rhythm of the bass reached every corner of the huge auditorium, and the energetic music could be heard from everywhere on the school's grounds.

Zahra entered the gymnasium alone from the main double doors and was greeted by a couple of members from the student body committee. One of them, a stocky boy that Zahra didn't know, affixed a sparkling paper bracelet to her wrist after verifying her name.

"Have a nice time," he said, smiling at her.

"Thanks," Zahra said nervously, looking past him at the spectacular display.

She immediately spotted DJ, his tall, lanky frame standing out next to the punch bowls. Her new friends from the Magic Club stood awkwardly in a half circle around him, a variety of drinks and snacks in their hands.

Zahra strode over to them, her senses assaulted by the sights, sounds, and smells of the transformed gymnasium. The colorful bulbs from the D.J. booth cut through the room's subdued lighting to paint several small clusters of dancers in shades of alternating blue, green, red, purple, and yellow. A row of chaperones on the other side of the room stood watching, looking like football referees on the sidelines waiting to spring at any inappropriate conduct. Zahra could pick out her algebra teacher, Mr. Ryan, among the chaperones, his round spectacles flashing colorfully in time with the D.J.'s light stands. The sight of him immediately made Zahra think of the midterm coming up in a couple of weeks, and she felt the knot in her stomach tighten, her nerves about attending the Winter Formal compounded by her apprehension about her exams. She shook her head and continued towards her friends, and was blasted by a wave of perfume emanating from a group of seniors that glided past her.

DJ raised his hand towards her as she approached the semicircle, mouthing something that Zahra couldn't hear over the thumping bass.

"What?" she yelled.

"Nice shirt!" DJ repeated, pointing at her *kameez*. Zahra could tell that he had dressed in earnest for the dance, replacing his customary print t-shirt and designer jeans with a short-sleeve plaid button-up shirt and skinny black slacks that were tucked into shiny black boots.

"Oh, thank you," Zahra mumbled, looking at her feet.

"What?!"

"I said thank you!"

DJ gave her the thumbs-up and continued his conversation with Bridget, who wore a long, flower-print A-line dress that was flattering on her curvy body. She leaned her forearms on her crutches and dexterously shuffled a deck of cards, trying to explain something to DJ over the noise.

"Here," Angie shuffled over from near the food table, dressed in a long-sleeved beige romper, and handed her a clear plastic glass filled with blue punch. Zahra smiled at her, taking a sip from the cup, and immediately regretting it. It tasted like blue paint looked, mixed with flat soda and something that smelled like sweat.

The rest of the odd little group stood off to the side, not quite on the dance floor, but not engaged in the tableside conversation either. Tamba and Tayo, both wearing brown khakis and black polos with forest green cardigans tied around their shoulders, danced in time with the music alongside Theo, who was himself a sight to be seen. The gangly teenager sported his baggy magician's outfit, his coattails swinging wildly behind him as he hopped from one foot to the other with no regard for the beat. What he lacked in skill he more than made up for with enthusiasm, and he held a tall top hat in one hand and a fistful of jelly beans in the other.

"How's it going?" Angie asked loudly.

"Fine," Zahra replied uncertainly. She hadn't been to a dance before, and wasn't sure what her behavior should be. Should she seek out Vazir, or wait for him? What would they do once they found each other? Was she supposed to stay until the Winter Formal was over?

She shifted her *kameez* uncomfortably, realizing that she was sweating, and that the room felt hot and stuffy to her. She took another sip of the punch, and although it was still repulsive, it seemed to settle her stomach a little.

"Do you like dancing?" Angie was saying.

Zahra shook her head. "Not really," she shouted.

Angie nodded her approval. "Me neither!"

The little group continued that way for some time, Zahra chatting with Angie and watching Bridget instruct DJ on a new trick, which resulted in an accidental spray of cards when DJ tried to emulate his new mentor's instructions.

As time passed, Zahra felt the anxiety inside of her building, cresting every few minutes or so and crashing against her frail confidence every time she looked at the gym's entrance or across the dance floor at Mr. Ryan. She had begun to worry that Vazir might not actually be coming to the Winter Formal at all, and felt like she couldn't focus on any of her friends' conversations with all of the noise and flashing lights buffeting her from different directions.

"Hey," she heard someone say, and turned towards the sound.

Zahra's agitated mind swept through a range of emotions at the sight, from elation, to disappointment, to curiosity. Joining her group was a handsome Caucasian American boy, dressed sportily in form-fitting jeans and a track jacket.

Across from Zahra, DJ looked up from his card trick. His brow furrowed with confusion, but his eyes sparkled underneath.

"Jason," he said breathlessly. "You came!"

Jason smiled shyly and nodded. "I…I wanted to…" DJ's sometimes-boyfriend stuffed his hands into the pockets of his jacket. "Can we talk?"

DJ looked at Bridget, who nodded. Zahra had the embarrassing feeling that she and her friends were watching an extremely private conversation unfold. DJ handed the deck of cards to Bridget, and gave Zahra a look that said, *we'll talk about this later.* He joined Jason and the couple disappeared through one of the gym's doors that had been left open for ventilation.

Zahra smiled, silently wishing that her friend and his would-be significant other were working things out between them. Then she glanced towards the main entrance for the hundredth time, disappointment at Vazir's absence threatening to sour her mood once again.

It wasn't until an hour after Zahra had arrived at the Winter Formal that her date materialized. Tamba, Tayo, and Theo had finally fully committed to their private dance party, and had moved in front of the D.J. booth where someone was handing out glowing pink and green necklaces. Angie and Bridget had excused themselves to use the ladies' room, and DJ was presumably off somewhere with Jason. Zahra remained alone, a bundle of nerves by the food table, her vision alternating between the psychedelic display of neon necklaces and flashing lights and something else, something darker, creeping at the edge of her eyesight. Her undergarments were drenched in sweat, and she felt flush, her lack of sleep and prolonged nervousness catching up with her.

Vazir entered the gym with a small entourage

of his friends, who peeled off towards the dance floor after they received their identification bracelets. Zahra's date sauntered over to her, having seen her as easily from the entryway as Zahra had spotted DJ. In the back of her mind, some small part of Zahra's nervous consciousness curiously realized that her traditional South Asian garb must have stood out against all of the Western outfits and decorations. She fidgeted with a bag of gummy polar bears that she had hoped would settle her roiling stomach, and forgot to smile as Vazir approached.

The young man's brown eyes lit up as he took in Zahra's appearance. "You look very nice," Vazir said in his slightly accented voice, raised to reach her over the music.

Zahra opened her mouth to speak, but found it dry, and tasting like ash. A wave of heat washed over her.

"Thank you," she managed. The extended wait had done a number on her jitters, and Vazir's image began to sway in her vision.

He was dressed immaculately. Dark green khakis hugged his muscular legs tightly, and he had chosen a pinstriped black button-up that accentuated his dark features. A stunning gold-plated watch on his left wrist completed the ensemble, and he wore black chukkas that made him stand a couple of inches taller than Zahra.

"Do you want to dance?" he asked, reaching out a hand towards her.

Something shifted in Zahra's exhausted, besieged mind, and a shadow fell across her eyes. On the surface, she saw Vazir, smiling and extending his hand in invitation, and a group of students behind him staring at her. Part of her knew that she must have looked unwell, as the students began pointing at her and holding their faces, and Vazir's expression quickly turned from merriment to concern.

The shadow across her vision grew deeper, and she saw within it, interposed upon Vazir's image, a being made from fire reaching out to point at her with one of its limbs. Its eyes were Vazir's eyes, and its arm was Vazir's flesh. Behind Vazir, the students were no longer students, but had the likeness of shadows roiling forth from a dark, endless portal.

Zahra's vision began to tunnel, and all sound ceased within the gymnasium. Time stopped, and reason escaped. In the dual image of Vazir and the fire spirit, Zahra could see the reflection of her own expression in Vazir's brown orbs, which were widening in horror. A figure wreathed in flame pointed back at him from Zahra's eyes, framed by an oblong portal that spit out darkness and shadow.

Ana siddiquki.

Zahra ran.

Time and direction had lost all meaning, and Zahra couldn't make sense of the sights and sounds that assailed her. She vaguely saw certain landmarks as she passed them, but she ran for the most part blindly, stumbling through the darkness across a field bathed in crimson. Shadowy whispers echoed throughout her hearing and blocked out all other sound. Pieces of her fractured consciousness recalled familiar sights like forgotten dreams, and streetlights, houses, and crosswalks flew by her unnoticed.

At long last, she came to the gate of her family's home, and she felt as though a pitcher of water had doused her from a great height. Her vision swam again, and she tore at the gate, panting towards the front door, her flat shoes flapping against the brick path underneath. She shivered, her sight and hearing suddenly returning to normal and leaving a void of sensation in their wake. She fumbled with her keys, her hands wet with perspiration and tears streaming down her face, unlocking the door clumsily and almost falling into the quiet house when it opened.

Zahra stood in the entryway, sobbing, her chest heaving. She closed the door quietly behind her and allowed her keys to drop to the floor, scuffing off her shoes. The house was dark save for a small light source in the living room, and Zahra padded towards it like a moth drawn to a flame.

Her father was there, standing next to his recliner with a book in his hand. A tall lamp provided just enough illumination for him to finish whatever chapter he had been reading, and his white undershirt and cotton pajama pants indicated that he was heading to bed.

He looked up as she came to the entrance of the room, and whatever barrier had been between them for the preceding week was melted in an instant. His face fell at the sight of her, and his brow was etched with concern.

"What's the matter, *beta*?" he asked softly.

Zahra choked on her tears, and ran to him. He dropped his book on the recliner and embraced her as she wept into his chest, fresh droplets staining his undershirt unnoticed.

"There, there, *beta*," Zahra's father cooed, holding her close to him and rubbing her head gently through her headscarf. "It's going to be OK."

5

The next day was better and worse for Zahra. For the first time in weeks, she woke up refreshed, having slept through the night with only a few flashes of her familiar sanguine dreamscape. Her mother, hearing the commotion in the living room upon Zahra's return, had joined her father in consoling their daughter after the terrible evening that she had experienced. Unsure of the nature of the experience herself, Zahra described it as a panic attack, which she knew DJ's older brother struggled with sometimes. Her parents were warm and understanding, their earlier apprehension about her attending the Winter Formal simultaneously forgotten and in a way affirmed. For the time being, they hadn't re-iterated their initial concerns, and Zahra had been grateful for their unconditional support.

Returning to school was difficult, for the most part because of Zahra's preconditioned sensitivity to drawing any more attention to herself than that which she had become accustomed to. As far as political leanings went, *Golden Mountain High School* was a bit more moderate than the very liberal surrounding Bay Area, and she was used to receiving curious looks because of her *hijab*. She had very little recollection of what had actually transpired between herself and Vazir the previous night, or those who had witnessed it. For his part, her date had texted her to inquire about her health, and Zahra had responded to let him know she was OK. She dreaded another encounter with him so soon after the Winter Formal, having no idea what she would say to him or if it would trigger another otherworldly experience.

Zahra was able to keep up in Algebra II with DJ, who was enthusiastic about the night that he'd had but concerned about Zahra's disappearance. According to the snippets of conversation they were able to sneak in between their problem sets — and glares from Mr. Ryan — DJ and Jason had walked the school's grounds, away from the dancing. Jason had explained to DJ that he had come out to his parents about his sexuality, and although they didn't seem to understand it, they were nonetheless supportive. The action had been liberating for him, and he described the exchange in great detail to DJ as they sat in the school's parking lot while eating sugar cookies from the Winter Formal. When they finally returned to the dance floor, Zahra had already disappeared, and DJ was only able to glean from their Magic Club friends that they heard she looked unwell, and left.

It was difficult for Zahra to explain to DJ what

had happened without unloading all of the details of her dreams in the busy classroom, so she told him simply that she hadn't been feeling well, and would fill him in later. It was a true statement, but Zahra felt badly about not being able to speak honestly with her closest confidant. She resolved to talk it through with him after school that evening, or on the weekend.

It being Friday, Zahra skipped lunch and took the BART train to Walnut Creek, a neighboring town which had the largest *masjid* east of the Caldecott Tunnel, called *Masjid al-Ihsan*. Like most *masajid*, *Masjid al-Ihsan* offered community prayers on Friday, considered to be a holy day in Zahra's tradition. Her attendance was about as regular as her adherence to her five daily prayers, in that although she understood its importance, she also accepted that her busy schedule only allowed her to participate on special occasions. She generally visited with her family on holidays like *'Eid*, but would venture out by herself now and then if she felt that she needed an added dose of spiritual stability.

Masjid al-Ihsan was an inviting one-story building that had been converted from a storefront a couple of blocks away from Walnut Creek's small business district. It was in many ways nondescript, featuring only a few hanging decorations on the wall outside that displayed curvilinear Arabic calligraphy in tones of black and green. A sign hung above the metal and plaster entryway that read simply:

Masjid al-Ihsan
Where All Are Welcome

In all other ways, the brick building was unadorned but clean, and could have once been a shoe shop or a tailor.

The interior of the *masjid* was an entirely different story. Non-load bearing walls had been taken down to create one large, open room covered in olive and cream carpets that were soft underfoot. The carpet colors alternated horizontally, providing natural rows that allowed congregants to line up for prayer while facing the direction of the *Ka'aba*. Framed pieces of Islamic calligraphy adorned the walls and hung from the ceiling, and a small wooden pulpit sat at the far end of the room, flanked by bookshelves that contained all manner of scriptures, including holy books from other traditions.

Zahra sat among the women in the room, listening to the sermon provided by the *imam* from the pulpit. The carpet underneath her had a calming effect on her exposed feet and hands, and she dug into it absently as she tried to listen to the homily. Her mind wandered, half-hearing the sermon, which was about the importance of faith and public service in one's daily life, and half-ruminating on fire spirits and portals. When the homily was complete, the group stood as one to enact the communal prayers together, reciting the Arabic verses and prostrating in unison, following the direction of the *imam* in front.

After the prayer, the women around Zahra congratulated each other with blessings and began to catch up on the goings-on of the past week. Some of the regulars moved to the back of the room and set up a small station with sweets and black tea, receiving small donations for the *masjid* from congregants leaving the building. Zahra waited until most of the *masjid* had cleared out, and moved to the head of the room to speak with the *imam*, who was finishing up some of his own personal prayers.

The *imam* turned as she approached, sitting half-cross-legged on a green and yellow prayer rug that was similar to Zahra's at home. He smiled at her, finishing mouthing a silent prayer while counting on a wooden *tasbih* in his right hand.

He was Moroccan, if Zahra remembered correctly, and had olive-brown skin that looked weathered on his exposed face and hands. A great, bushy beard that was more grey than black tugged at his jaw, and thick eyebrows poked out over kind-looking eyes that had laugh lines at their corners. He wore a long, sand-colored *djellaba* and sky-blue linen pants, and a lime green turban was wrapped expertly around the top of his head.

"*As-salaamu 'aleykum,*" Zahra said politely, using her best Arabic and sitting down at a polite distance from the *imam*. A faint aroma of sandalwood teased her nostrils.

"*Wa 'aleykum as-salaam*, young lady," the *imam* returned, smiling. His Arabic accent was perfect, and his English less so, but Zahra knew from his sermons that he was fluent in both languages. "What can I do for you?"

Zahra hesitated, not quite certain what had motivated her to speak with the *imam*, but instinctively comfortable trusting him and his knowledge. In their very brief interactions during holiday gatherings, he had always been kind to her and her family. She took a deep breath and spoke her mind.

"*Shaykh*," she began, using his honorific title, "I have been having some bad dreams and wondered if there is some sort of *du'a* that I can recite that will help me?"

The *imam* looked at her compassionately, his eyebrows raising in concern. "I am sorry to hear that. What kind of dreams are you having?"

Zahra glanced down at the *tasbih*, the wooden beads still moving under the *imam*'s brown fingers. "It's...hard to describe. I think it may be silly."

The *imam* said nothing, patiently waiting for Zahra to proceed.

"Do you..." she said haltingly, looking back up at him. "Have you ever seen any of those fantasy movies, with fire people and shadow creatures?"

The *imam*'s eyebrows raised even further.

"Fire creatures!" he exclaimed. *"Mithl al-jinnah?"*

Zahra shook her head, not understanding.

"Al-jinnah?" The *imam* asked again. He seemed to be searching for the English word. "Jinns?"

Something vaguely familiar nagged at one of Zahra's distant memories. "I don't know, I think so?"

The *imam* nodded, his beard wagging with the motion. "In our tradition, there are humans, angels, and jinns. Humans were made from earth, angels from light, and jinns from fire. Have you been dreaming about jinns?"

Zahra pursed her lips, considering. "I guess so?" Emboldened by the *imam*'s understanding, she explained briefly the setup of the recurring dream, including the ruby moon and the grassy plain, capping it off with a description of the fire spirit pointing towards her. She deliberately left out the piece about the gaping portal and its denizens, not wanting to press her luck.

The *imam* nodded along with her explanation, and sat thoughtfully when she had finished. After a moment, he reached into a pocket of his *djellaba* and produced a small, wrist-sized circlet of *tasbih*, handing it to Zahra. It was made from jade-colored round stones, and had an elastic band that would expand over one's hand to fit most wrist sizes.

"If you ask most people here about *al-jinnah*," he said, waving his free hand towards the

68

mostly empty *masjid*, "you won't find out much about them. People don't study them because they don't want to know anything outside of their normal world. But there is another world—*al-Akhira*—which is different from this world.

"Some people can see into that world, and they become crazy. Other people can only hear it, or they dream about it. Like you." The *imam* pointed at Zahra, nodding to himself again.

"Some people can even *talk* to the angels, or to the jinns," he continued. "*Tatakallum ma'a al-jinnah.*"

"*Tatakallum?*" Zahra repeated haltingly.

"*Ma'a al-jinnah,*" the *imam* finished for her. "Speaking, with the jinns. Jinnspeak."

Zahra's eyes narrowed, her mind trying to wrap around the *imam*'s words. "Jinnspeak."

"Jinnspeak," he said again, with finality. His accent made the word sound like *jinn-es-peak*. "It is a good dream, meaning that you are seeing beyond this world, *al-Dunya*, and into the other world, *al-Akhira*. Maybe the jinn is trying to tell you something."

Zahra nodded, feeling many different gears in her mind come together with a new understanding, or at least a new name, for her dreamscapes.

"So," she said slowly, playing with the green *tasbih* in her hand, "what should I do?"

"Listen," the *imam* said, gravity in his voice. "Listen to whatever your companion is trying to tell you. And make *du'a*," he pointed at the *tasbih* in her hand. "Pray for guidance and counsel."

"OK, I can do that," Zahra said, heartened for the first time in weeks. She smiled at the *imam*, and felt like hugging him. "Thank you, *Shaykh*."

The *imam* smiled again, his white teeth peeking out from under the bushy beard. "You're welcome, young lady. See you next week?"

Zahra stood up from her seated position, shaking out her legs, which had fallen asleep. She gave him a sheepish look. "I'll try," she said.

The *imam* waggled his eyebrows knowingly. "I'll see you then."

Zahra began to leave, and then thought of something. She turned back to the *imam*, who had already started folding his prayer rug.

"*Shaykh*," she queried, "what does *ana siddiquki* mean?"

The *imam* looked at her quizzically. "*Siddiquka*," he corrected. "If you're saying it to me, it's *siddiquka*, because I am a man. If I say it to you, it is *siddiquki*."

"*Ana siddiquka*," Zahra repeated, pointing towards the *imam*. Then she gestured towards herself. "*Ana siddiquki*."

The *imam* nodded his approval. "That is correct."

"What is the translation?"

The *imam*'s face lit up, his crow's feet etching

merry brown lines at the corners of his eyes. "Oh! *Ana siddiquki*. It means, 'I am your friend.'"

*****

Zahra took the BART back to *GMHS* and cornered DJ in the hallway that afternoon in between their classes.

"Tell me everything you know about *Warlords of Gunthor*," she accosted him, grabbing him by the elbow.

DJ looked surprised. "Since when do you want to learn about video games?"

Zahra shook her head. "Not all video games, just *Warlords*," she said. "Particularly whatever you know about portals."

The two friends made a date to meet at *Ground Rules* after DJ's Friday afternoon swim meet. Ever the student, Zahra showed up to the neighborhood cafe with a pencil and scratch pad, ready to take notes. The cafe was quiet, with only a few patrons sitting and enjoying the dying afternoon light before the evening crowd bustled in.

DJ was already waiting for her, sipping at his customary iced chocolate and fiddling with his phone. His blonde hair was slicked back against his head, still wet from swimming.

Zahra bought a pastry from the cafe counter, having sworn herself off of green tea for the foreseeable future, remembering all too vividly the sequence of events that had ensued the previous time she had ordered the beverage. She plopped down across from DJ, who continued to tinker with his phone.

"Hey," she said, opening her notebook and stuffing an oversized piece of pastry into her mouth.

"Sup," DJ replied, finally looking up from his phone. *"Warlords?"*

Zahra nodded, her mouth too full to respond.

DJ put his phone face down on the table, leaning forward eagerly. "OK. *Warlords of Gunthor* is a fantasy massively multiplayer online roleplaying game set in a land called Arturia..."

"I know what an MMORPG is, DJ," Zahra said reproachfully around a mouthful of pastry.

DJ gave her a pained look. "Do you want my help, or not?"

"Sorry."

"The world has two different factions — the Angiri, and the Zeherim — who are in a constant battle for rulership over Arturia. The Angiri are descended from angels, and the Zeherim from demons."

Zahra wiped her hand on a napkin and started scribbling in her notebook. "So the Zeherim are the bad guys?"

DJ shook his head. "Not exactly. Both factions have good characters and bad characters, but they're at war with each other. So if you're playing an Angiri character, you can fight the Zeherim, and vice versa."

"What kind of character do you play?"

"Blood Sorcerer," DJ said proudly. "I've also got a Shield Warrior, Forest Ranger, Fire Mage…"

Zahra perked up at that. "Fire Mage?"

DJ nodded, grabbing his phone and pulling up some screenshots of his characters through an app. "In *Warlords*, you pick your faction, and then the race of your character, and then your class. My Blood Sorcerer is an elf." He showed Zahra a picture of a blue-skinned, fey-looking character with pointed ears and a long red robe, holding a gem-encrusted staff.

Zahra squinted at the picture. "What's a class?"

DJ flipped through some pictures on his phone. "It's basically your specialty. Like my Blood Sorcerer, who uses dark magic to attack other characters, or Theo's Water Shaman, who has these water totems…"

"What's that one?" Zahra asked as DJ scrolled past one of his characters.

Her friend flipped back to what looked like a humanoid wizard with stylized orange flames in place of its hair and eyes. Zahra vaguely remembered seeing the character on DJ's phone the night her dreams first began. "That's my Fire Mage. I call him 'Burns.'"

"What kind of race is he?"

DJ spread his fingers on the phone's screen to zoom in on the character's face. "Djinnborn.

They're descended from genies."

"Jinns?" Zahra asked.

DJ shrugged. "I dunno. Is that some Arabic thing?"

Zahra bit at the eraser of her pencil, thinking. "I think so? I'm not sure."

DJ made an exasperated sound, frustrated. "Will you tell me what this is about? I don't get why you all of a sudden want to know all of this stuff."

Zahra grimaced, chastised. "Sorry," she said. "I haven't been myself for the past couple of weeks." She launched into the story of her dreamscapes, allowing her thoughts and descriptions to flow freely. In some way, the events of the Winter Formal had released her reservations of talking about her problems with others, as though the worst had already happened, and she now had nothing to lose. Her afternoon talk with the *imam* had boosted her confidence, as well.

When she finished, DJ sat back in his chair, pursing his lips in thought. His hair had dried, slowly regaining its shaggy consistency.

"So you think it's some kind of genie trying to tell you something?" he mused.

"Jinn," Zahra corrected, "but yeah."

DJ nodded, considering. "But what's the moon about? And the grass plain?"

"I have no idea," Zahra said. "But you and Theo said something about portals in *Warlords*."

"Yeah, so," DJ replied, "Arturia is ruled by a

High Council of Archmagi…"

"Who?"

"Like, really powerful wizards, from both the Angiri and the Zeherim. The number of spots on the Council per faction depends on how much that faction is dominating the other in combat."

Zahra nodded slowly, understanding. "And you're Angiri?"

DJ made a disgusted sound. "As *if* I'd join those chumps. All of my characters are Zeherim."

"And how do the portals fit in?"

"Right. When you create a character in *Warlords*, you choose a race and class, and then you can go questing in the world by yourself, or join up with other people and run dungeons, fight raid bosses, and stuff like that."

"Like your guild?" Zahra asked cautiously, wanting to get it right.

DJ's eyes lit up with approval. "Right! My guild is called Text Calibur. It's a play on one of the game's main story quests, which is based on…"

"DJ, focus!" Zahra chided.

"Sorry. When you're in a guild of twenty or more players, you can try to fight these really difficult raid bosses, which gets you loot like armor and weapons. But more importantly, defeating them swings the battle in favor of your faction, eventually getting you more Archmagi on the Council."

Zahra felt her tenuous grip on the game's concepts slipping. She tried to steer the conversation back into familiar territory. "And you go through portals?"

DJ shook his head, taking a sip of iced chocolate. "You close them. The raid bosses open portals, which are like magical gates. Their minions come out of them and you have to fight them, which is why you need so many people to attempt a raid. A bunch of your guild members have to fight the minions, while another group has to attack the boss, and while all that's happening, someone else has to close the portal."

Understanding began to dawn as Zahra continued to take notes from DJ's explanation. She began thinking out loud, scribbling as she talked.

"So the Angiri and Zeherim are at war with one another, and have a number of seats on the High Council of Archmagi based on how well they're doing in battle."

"Correct."

"And players can form guilds to fight raid bosses, who open portals so their creatures can come out and fight you."

"Right."

"And one of your characters is a jinn Fire Mage?"

"Djinnborn, but yeah."

"Hmm." Zahra tapped her pencil against the table in between them, half of her pastry sitting forgotten on a napkin next to her. She adjusted the new jade *tasbih* on her wrist idly, trying to fit the puzzle pieces into some sort of logical pattern. "The Djinnborn thing makes me think the figure in my dream is somehow connected to *Warlords of Gunthor*, but I'm not sure how the moon or portals fit in."

DJ sipped thoughtfully at his cold drink, which was almost finished. A sizeable crowd had filtered into the cafe over the course of their discussion, and the room was becoming a little stuffy from the influx of bodies. "I don't know about the moon," he said at length, "but the portal in your dream does sound like something in *Warlords*."

Zahra nodded her agreement. "I think so too. But how?"

DJ's handsome face scrunched up in concentration, then relaxed suddenly as he came up with something. "Didn't Angie say something about the Occult Society and portals?"

Zahra chewed the corner of her lip, thinking. "Yeah...what did Bridget call them?"

"'Weird,'" DJ replied. "Like that flier they posted on the bulletin board." They both squirmed in their chairs a little as they remembered the writhing, curvilinear script of the postcard. "I think they meet on Mondays."

"Davis Library," Zahra murmured, recalling the location on the flier. She shivered. "Do you think we should try asking them?"

"I guess," DJ said dubiously, finishing his drink and placing it on the table with a clink. He looked intrigued by Zahra's story and its connection with *Warlords of Gunthor*, but clearly didn't like the idea of meeting with the mysterious Occult Society any more than she did. He shrugged. "What could it hurt?"

6

Zahra spent the weekend studying for her midterms, which were coming up in less than two weeks. The Algebra II test would undoubtedly be the most difficult one for her, and she met with DJ every day to go over problem sets and chat about *Warlords of Gunthor*. Occasionally, one or two of their new friends from the Magic Club would join them, and although they didn't share any mutual classes, Zahra was grateful for a new group of study partners who made the dreary work more interesting.

Monday's classes came and went, and Zahra's teachers had kicked their midterm preparation into high gear. Zahra appreciated the review, particularly in Algebra II, and felt like she was slowly starting to understand some of the more complex concepts and able to reproduce them. It helped that her energy was steadily returning, and her sleep becoming more regular. Since the Winter Formal, she had still dreamed every night of the fiery figure on the ruby plain, but had begun to conceptualize the dream as a scene from *Warlords of Gunthor* rather than a frightening reality. It was just as vivid and intense, but Zahra was able to accept the flamewalker as a friend that meant her no harm. She began to try to identify and memorize details within the dreamscape to better decipher what her fiery companion was trying to tell her, hoping that such an approach would lead to some sort of resolution.

On Monday afternoon, Zahra met DJ at the entrance to the Davis Library, a newly renovated building towards the rear of the campus grounds. It stood apart from the rest of *GMHS'* structures, sharing a wall with the gigantic gymnasium. Ever the punctual one, DJ was already waiting for her at the open double doors.

"Ready?" he asked as she walked up. A pair of headphones sat lazily around his collar.

"I guess," Zahra hemmed.

The library had a small, wood-framed antechamber, with a circulation desk that allowed students to return books and make inquiries about reference material. A pair of magnetized security panels flanked the pathway into the library's main atrium, ensuring that students had to check out their books through the circulation desk. The pathway ran a circle around the atrium, which in turn had rows of books leading away perpendicularly towards the edges of the building. A stairway led down to the second level of the atrium, which contained more books and a handful of study rooms. The building had a pleasant scent of paper and cedar wood, along with the hushed feeling that only a room full of books could produce.

Zahra and DJ walked together down the stairs, assuming that the *Occult Society* would be meeting in one of the study rooms. They made their way around the underground level's maze of books to the very rear of the building, which housed a series of cubicles, and where several students had begun their bi-yearly ritual of cramming for midterms. Two rooms were built into the library wall, with simple frosted windows and wooden doors that hid their contents from view. Both doors had small whiteboards affixed to their fronts, and one read simply, in handwritten cursive: *Occult Society*.

"I guess this is it," Zahra said, gesturing towards the door.

"I guess so," her friend echoed, placing his hand on the metal door handle. They exchanged a glance, and DJ suddenly pulled out his phone and held it out in front of him like a talisman warding off evil. Taking a deep breath, he opened the door into the small room.

Zahra initially wasn't quite sure what she was looking at. The room's overhead lights were on, bathing the area in harsh fluorescence, but there was a portable blacklight set up on a desk pointing towards a large dry erase board, illuminating a complex diagram drawn in orange, green, and purple. Four students stood around the room or sat in chairs, glancing up in alarm as DJ opened the door. At first glimpse, they all looked identical, wearing matching black t-shirts that had a light green bullseye pattern pasted onto their fronts. At the center of the insignia's concentric circles was a strange symbol that Zahra didn't recognize.

A fifth student stood in front of the dry erase board, several markers in his hand. The blacklight gave him an eerie look, darkening his skin and hair but casting his teeth and eyes in a ghastly white radiance. The bullseye on his shirt glowed phosphorescently in the dark light. His eyes stared daggers at DJ and Zahra as they burst into the room, and he made a slicing motion in the air with one hand towards one of the other students.

"Cut it," he said sharply.

Dutifully, the student he addressed flipped a switch on the blacklight. The room returned to its normal brightness, and the writing on the board disappeared. The boy with the markers squinted with the change in light, and although his features had returned to a normal human color, the ghostly image of his eyes and teeth still burned in Zahra's vision.

"We've got this room until five o'clock," he said curtly, misunderstanding the newcomers' intent.

"No," DJ said quickly. Having seen that there wasn't any present danger, he slipped his phone back into his pocket. "We're just here because...are you the Occult Society?"

Zahra scanned the room a second time,

noticing that the students were indeed dressed similarly, but were definitely not identical. *GMHS* was a big school, and although she thought she recognized a couple of them, she didn't know any of them personally. Two of them stood out to her because of their platinum-dyed short hair, causing Zahra to belatedly recognize that they were separate people. She had always seen one or the other around campus and, because of their similar features, assumed they were the same person.

The student at the head of the class, who seemed to be their leader, made a clucking sound with his tongue. "We are. What do you want?" he said rudely.

"We'd like to ask you a few questions," Zahra stepped in, not liking the tone he was taking with her friend.

The leader turned his gaze towards her, and it was like looking into the eyes of a shark. They were a deep shade of brown, almost black, and cold. His cheek twitched. "We're not taking new members," he said with finality.

"But," DJ stammered, "we saw a postcard on the bulletin board..."

The head student shifted his glare away from Zahra, leaving her with a shiver. He looked at one of the sitting students, his ire palpable in the small room.

"Didn't I tell you to remove the fliers?"

The student shifted in her seat, evidently uncomfortable under the boy's stare. She had long red hair and freckles that made her look almost sunburned in the harsh light. "Sorry, I thought I got all of them," she replied meekly.

"It's my fault," said the boy who was still standing by the blacklight. He wore a camouflage baseball cap that matched his cargo pants, and had a thick nose ring that marred an otherwise unremarkable complexion. "I was supposed to get the hallway fliers."

The leader harrumphed, his expression softening by a tiny fraction as he turned back towards Zahra and DJ. "We're not taking new members," he repeated. "Come back next semester. We might have some new openings then."

Zahra and DJ nodded as one, turning on their heels and closing the door behind them. They raced together back through the lower level of the atrium and up the stairs, through the security panels and out through the double doors.

It wasn't until the afternoon sun touched their faces that Zahra exhaled, realizing that she had been holding her breath.

*****

Zahra and DJ immediately left *GMHS* and made a bee-line for *Ground Rules*, a silent agreement passing between them that whatever they had just witnessed was too strange to be discussed openly on school property. As soon as they made it to the cafe and ordered their drinks, they sat down in a huff, having half-walked, half-run the short distance from school.

"What the *heck* was that?" Zahra said, wiping her forehead with a napkin. She adjusted her headscarf, tucking a few loose hairs back within its soft cloth.

"Man, I dunno," DJ replied, taking a deep breath and exhaling through pursed lips. He sized up his full glass of iced chocolate like a cat considering a mouse, and then took a huge gulp.

"It's like," Zahra mused, stirring a new concoction of soda water, raspberry syrup, and lemon slices with a straw. "It's like they were planning something, but they didn't want us to see it?"

"Yeah," DJ agreed, wiping a chocolate moustache off his lip with the back of his hand. "Those blacklight pens are a neat trick."

"And what about those shirts?" Zahra said, remembering the weird bullseye insignias. "Bridget was right, those kids *are* weird."

DJ took another swig of chocolate, crushing ice between his teeth. "Yeah," he said again. "That leader guy gives me the creeps."

Zahra sipped her drink through the straw. It was almost too sweet, making her jaws clench involuntarily. "I wish we knew what they were hiding. Those diagrams looked crazy."

Her friend raised his eyebrows over the iced chocolate glass, which was almost vertical as he drained the rest of his drink in one sip. He sighed contentedly, putting the glass down and licking his lips.

"I got it," he said.

Zahra gave him a confused look. "Got what?"

"The diagram. I grabbed it before they turned off the blacklight."

"I don't understand."

DJ pulled his phone out of his pocket, pressing its little "home" button twice and showing it to Zahra. A camera app popped up instantaneously.

"I had a weird feeling right before we went in there," he explained, "like they might have a goat tied up there or something. I'm not sure what I expected."

He swiped a finger across the screen, and the motion brought up a gallery of pictures and screenshots. He tapped the most recent one, which expanded to show the scene that they had just witnessed. It was a little blurry, and the phone's camera didn't seem to appreciate the multiple light sources in the picture, but the dry erase board diagram was at least recognizable. The Occult Society leader's face and body were mired in shadow, his white-green eyes and teeth floating supernaturally in midair.

Zahra ignored the creepy image of the student and focused on the diagram. She reached over the table and spread her fingers across the screen to zoom in on the dry erase board.

"It looks like a bunch of numbers and shapes."

DJ nodded, squinting along with her. *"Mmm hmm. Maybe they're color coded?"*

Zahra stared at the diagram, trying to piece together any semblance of understanding. There was a sequence of ascending green numbers, all of which had purple slashes through them, and what looked like an orange circle. There was also a purple caricature of the same insignia that was on the Occult Society's t-shirts, with a bunch of cryptic symbols placed around it in a pentagonal shape.

"What's that?" Zahra asked, pointing at the insignia.

DJ frowned. "That's weird," he said. "It's the Symbol of Gunthor."

Zahra looked closely at the emblem. Upon closer inspection, it had the appearance of an oval, with a vortex swirling between its lines. Four claws gripped the exterior of the oval on opposing sides. "Like, the game logo?" she asked dubiously. She had seen DJ wear several different *Warlords of Gunthor* t-shirts, and none of them looked like the insignia in question.

"No," DJ said, "the actual symbol of the High Council of the Archmagi. Like, what they wear on their robes in the game. I've never seen it anywhere else."

"What does it mean?"

DJ shrugged. "It's kind of like a reference to when you close a portal while fighting a raid boss."

Something slippery snaked its way around Zahra's spine. She didn't like the direction the conversation was heading. "What are the other symbols?"

Her friend stared at the pentagram, trying to make sense of it. "They're other raid portal symbols. When you're fighting a raid boss, you have to actually interact with each one of the symbols to close the portal and defeat it."

Zahra guffawed. "Video games are weird."

DJ gave her a mild look over his phone. "And studying Spanish in your free time is cool?"

"Point taken." She looked at the symbol in the middle again. "Why would everyone be wearing the Symbol of Gunthor on their shirts?"

He shook his head, his shaggy hair moving wildly. "I didn't even notice." He pinched the screen to zoom out on the picture, bringing the Occult Society leader back into view. The bullseye logo shone clearly in iridescent green, floating below the boy's eyes and teeth.

Zahra shivered. The connection between her dreams, the portals, and DJ's game was too strong to ignore. "Do you think they're doing something with *Warlords*?"

"I have no idea," DJ said honestly. "These are definitely raid symbols, but not sure about the other stuff."

Zahra nodded, letting the information settle. She mixed her drink again, the syrup having settled at the bottom of the cup. "What about the numbers, and the circle thing?" She pointed at the orange disc.

"I dunno. The numbers definitely seem like they're in some order, but I can't place it."

"Hmm."

DJ turned off the screen of his phone and put it back in his pocket. He sat back in his chair, swirling the empty glass in front of him perfunctorily. "I could ask my guildmates about it," he offered.

Zahra made a face. As much as she trusted DJ, she didn't relish the idea of him discussing their admittedly wild conversation about her dreams with some online friends that she had never met.

DJ must have read her expression, and changed his tactic. "Or, we could talk to Theo. He plays *Warlords*."

Zahra nodded, remembering. "I guess so," she said slowly. She trusted her new friends a whole lot more than some randoms that she had only heard about from DJ. "I guess it wouldn't hurt to ask the Magic Club about the symbols. They might know something."

"Great," DJ said, letting out a deep breath through his nose. "Let's hope they know more than we do."

*****

The next day, Zahra and DJ met up with the Magic Club during their normal Tuesday lunch period, excited to share their experience visiting the Occult Society. Zahra was still trepidatious about revealing the full extent of her dreams to anyone other than DJ, but admitted to herself that they needed help putting together all of the different pieces.

Zahra began the conversation bluntly after the group finished practicing a complex new trick that involved Angie's mind-reading talents and Bridget's card skills to convince an audience member, played this time by Tayo, that they themselves were gifted with magical abilities.

"I need your help," Zahra said simply as Bridget cleaned up her cards from the teacher's desk and the others began eating a quick lunch before the class bell rang.

"What kind of help?" Angie asked, producing a sandwich from a paper bag that had her name written across it.

Zahra had no idea where to begin, and stared down at her own lunch in front of her. Her mother had packed a simple meal of cold chicken *kathi* rolls with a little container of pre-made tamarind chutney, and a small apple. She picked at the roll, mulling over the best way to ask her friends about the portals.

"I've been having these dreams," she began slowly, choosing her words carefully, "and I'm trying to figure out how they're related to some symbols we found from the Occult Society."

"What kind of dreams?" Tamba asked, sipping from a juice box.

Zahra took a deep breath, and gave the Magic Club a quick overview of her nightly visions, paying particular attention to her description of her fiery companion and the clarion that sounded after she was sucked into the shadowy portal.

The group listened to her story carefully, eating their lunches silently as the words poured out of Zahra. Angie was the first to speak.

"Before we dissect the dream, what are the symbols you mentioned earlier?"

"They're raid symbols, from *Warlords of Gunthor*," DJ offered, clearing his throat. Zahra was grateful that she had already discussed the dreams with DJ at length, feeling more confident having him in her corner.

"I don't play *Warlords*," Bridget said, putting the deck of cards in her zip-up jacket pocket. "What's a raid symbol?"

DJ looked at Zahra, who gestured at him to explain. Quickly, he described the game's setup, with Theo chiming in now and again with his own experience playing *Warlords of Gunthor*. The group picked up on the main concepts quickly, understanding that teams like DJ's guild could get together and tackle raid bosses, which involved fighting monsters and closing portals by interacting with symbols.

"I confirmed the symbols last night," DJ said. "They're set up in a pentagon around the raid portal. Someone has to go around clicking them to close the portal while the rest of the group fights the boss and its minions."

Theo nodded. "It's pretty tough, but most guilds can do it if they have enough people and know what they're doing."

"What does this have to do with the Occult Society?" Tayo asked, his sister nodding as if she had the same question.

DJ pulled up the picture on his phone, holding the screen out in front of him so the others could see the image of the diagram.

"We went and saw them yesterday," he explained. "They had all of these runes written in blacklight ink, with the Symbol of Gunthor in the middle and on these t-shirts they were wearing."

Zahra nodded. "They were all dressed the same and turned off the blacklight when we opened the door. It was weird."

"Didn't I warn you?" Bridget drawled.

Theo had a puzzled look on his long face. "What made you go to them in the first place?"

"Angie suggested it," Zahra said, a bit more accusatorily than she meant it. She felt like the thread of the conversation was slipping. "I'm not sure what to make of it, to be honest. It just seems like my dreams, *Warlords*, and the Occult Society are all connected somehow."

Angie wiped her mouth on a napkin, crumbling her paper bag and throwing it into a wastebasket next to the teacher's desk. She stood and walked over to Zahra, who was sitting in one of the student desks.

"Bridget, can you help me here?" she said, wiping crumbs from her hands.

Bridget slid out from behind her own desk and used her crutches to stalk over to them.

Zahra looked at the pair worriedly, concerned that she had offended Angie with her comment. The latter made a signal to Bridget, who took out her deck of cards and started shuffling them from one hand to the other in the air. Zahra felt her eyes drawn to the action, red-and-white play cards riffling like an accordion in between Bridget's plump and dexterous hands.

"Sometimes, in one of our mind-reading acts," Angie began, her voice shifting from its usual pleasant timbre to a sultry monotone, "we give an audience member a series of prompts and tell them to let their subconscious put together a story."

Zahra found herself mesmerized by the sound of the mind reader's voice, and the continuous ruffling of Bridget's cards had a calming effect on her body.

"What I want you to do," Angie droned, "is describe the dream to us again, but this time try to allow your subconscious to fill in the other pieces that you're not sure about."

Zahra nodded dumbly, feeling Angie's voice and Bridget's cards take over the burden she had been carrying for almost three weeks. A weight began to lift from her shoulders as she started speaking, her voice joining the shuffling cards as the only sounds in the quiet room.

"I'm standing on a field of grass, lit by a red moon," she spoke, seeing the images as she described them. "It's a place that feels familiar to me, and quiet, but I can hear the wind roaring in my ears at the same time. I turn around and see a fiery figure pointing at me.

"Or not *at* me," she corrected herself. "Behind me."

"Good," Angie's soft voice prompted her. "What's it pointing at?"

Zahra felt her eyes gloss over as she entered a dreamlike state, recalling. "A portal. It's dark, and scary, with all kinds of creatures trying to get out of it. I feel it pulling at me, sucking me in, sucking the *world* in…"

"*STOP.*" Angie's voice held the same calm monotone, but was suddenly full of command. Zahra's dream halted in the middle of her explanation, as though it were a video and Angie had hit the *pause* button. "What does the portal look like?"

"It's…" Zahra scanned her dreamscape, feeling her subconscious knitting together disparate pieces of information. "It's a big oval, with claws gripping it on the top and bottom." She licked her lips, her mouth dry. "It looks like the symbol on the Occult Society's t-shirts."

"The Symbol of Gunthor," she heard DJ say from somewhere far away.

"What's around it?" Angie droned. Zahra felt her dreamscape shift, her vision blurring for a moment, like she was a camera zooming out

94

from the scene she had been experiencing every night. She now witnessed it from a different angle, noticing for the first time a handful of symbols writhing on the ground near the portal.

"There are markings," Zahra said dreamily, examining them in her mind's eye. "They're spread out in a pentagon around the portal. They look like DJ's raid symbols."

"What's the fire figure doing?"

Zahra's vision blurred as the scene zoomed out even more, revealing a top-down view of her dream. Zahra saw herself, frightened and alone, staring at the symbol-ringed portal, dark creatures frozen in place as they clambered out of the oblong fissure. Behind her stood her jinn companion, its arm extended towards her and its flames licking motionlessly towards the red-rimmed horizon.

"It looks like DJ's Djinnborn Fire Mage, from *Warlords*. It's pointing towards me, or the portal," Zahra said, her breath catching. Something in the jinn's posture, viewed from this new angle, changed her perspective on the interaction.

"It's...warning me," she said, her subconscious fully taking over the explanation. "The Occult Society's going to do something with the *Warlords of Gunthor* portal, and the figure is warning me."

Something shifted in Zahra, like a key fitting into a lock and waiting to be turned. All at once, the dreamscape dissolved, spiraling in her vision and being replaced harshly with Angie's stern face hovering in front of her. She blinked, the bright lights of the classroom feeling foreign to her eyes.

"Well that was productive," Bridget said, slipping her cards back into her pocket.

"Works like a charm," Angie said confidently.

Zahra rubbed at her forehead. "So," she said, trying to shake her grogginess, "this whole thing is about *Warlords of Gunthor*? But I don't even play it. DJ does."

Angie shrugged, walking away from Zahra's desk to sit back down at her own. "Sometimes your subconscious picks up on small details that may not be the most obvious even if you're paying attention. It's pretty much the basis for every one of my mind reading tricks."

"But what would the Occult Society want to do with *Warlords*?" Tamba mused out loud.

"They obviously play it," DJ responded. "They all had t-shirts with the Symbol of Gunthor on them, and drew the raid symbol pentagram on the diagram."

"I can do some digging on them," Theo offered. "See if anyone online knows if they have a guild or something."

Angie nodded. "Wasn't there more to the diagram than those symbols?"

"Yeah," DJ said, bringing up the image on his phone again. "There are these numbers with slashes through them, and a big orange thing."

The little group crowded around DJ's phone,

looking at the jargon more carefully.

"That's not an orange, it's a moon," Zahra exclaimed breathlessly, Angie's hypnotization still lingering in her subconscious. "It's the full moon from my dream!"

"Full moon?" Bridget said disparagingly. "Could these guys be more cliché?"

"What about the slashed numbers?" DJ asked the group. "They seem to be progressively increasing in digits."

"I don't think they're slashes," Tamba said. "They look like dates, but in European notation."

Zahra looked at the numbers for the hundredth time, her vision clearing. They did seem to be increasing in a series, but followed the same format of one or two digits followed by a slash, followed by another one or two digits. Zahra had seen European date notation before, but wouldn't have recognized it as readily as would someone from another country, like the exchange students Tamba and Tayo.

"That makes sense," she said. "But dates for what?"

No one had an answer to that question, but the group seemed buoyed by their progress.

"So we've got something to go on," Angie summarized, taking charge of the situation. "The Occult Society's planning something to do with the portals from *Warlords*, and Zahra's subconscious has been warning her about it."

The Magic Club leader pointed at her head

illusionist. "Theo's going to look into their possible motives online, and whatever other information he can find. DJ," she shifted her gaze to Zahra's best friend, "can you try to figure out what the dates mean?"

"Sure."

Angie nodded her approval. "We know it has something to do with the full moon," she said. "Can someone figure out when the next one is?"

"I can do that," Tamba said.

"Good. So we'll find out motive and we'll find out time. What do we know about location?"

Zahra shook her head. "Not much. Just a grassy area, like an open plain."

"Sounds like the sports field," Tayo said. The whole group turned towards the soccer player, who had been quiet. He shrugged. "It's the only grassy area nearby."

"Isn't it closed?" Bridget asked, packing up her lunch in a blue and green knapsack.

"Yeah," he replied. The *GMHS* sports field had been undergoing renovations all semester, forcing the soccer team to practice in the gymnasium, which, Zahra knew from Tayo's occasional complaints, they hated.

"Can you check it out?" Angie asked.

"I'll go this afternoon," he said helpfully, rising from his seat as the classroom bell chimed.

Angie waited for the bell to stop ringing before addressing the group again. "OK, sounds like we've got our marching orders. Let's check back here on Thursday. And be careful," she said, picking up a black backpack and thrusting her arms through the straps. "We don't know what kind of danger Zahra's subconscious may have stumbled across."

7

For the first time in three weeks, Zahra felt like she was working towards something instead of flailing about without any direction. Her midterm preparations were steadily, if glacially, coming together, and she felt liberated by sharing the burden of puzzling through the meaning behind her dreams with the Magic Club.

In their Thursday meeting, Theo and DJ reported on their findings about the Occult Society's involvement in *Warlords of Gunthor*, which turned out to be extensive.

"They have their own guild," Theo related to the group, his pale features flush with excitement. "It's called Yteicos Tlucco."

"Yteicos Tlucco," Angie said, frowning as she tried to pronounce the strange words. "What's it mean?"

"It's just 'Occult Society' backwards," DJ explained.

"*Stupid*," Bridget groused.

"Yeah, not very creative," Theo continued. "I was able to run a dungeon with one of their guildmates, who also thinks they're kind of crazy."

"What did they say?" Zahra asked.

Theo made a face. "They're really into the lore behind the game, particularly around Gunthor. They talk a lot about this conspiracy theory where the world in *Warlords* is a mirror of Earth, and that the raid portals are actually sources of power."

Tamba scratched her head, her long curls bouncing playfully. "They *like* the portals? I thought the portals were supposed to be evil."

DJ nodded in response. "They are, and you're supposed to close them to defeat the raid bosses. But the Occult Society think that if you were to somehow open the portals, you'd be able to draw upon their power."

"And do what?" Tayo asked.

"Who knows," Theo said. "You can't do it in the game, so I'm not sure where they're getting their information from."

Angie changed the subject slightly. "What did you find out about the slashed numbers?"

"They *are* dates," DJ confirmed, smiling at Tamba and confirming her suspicions. She flashed a toothy grin in acknowledgment. "Apparently Yteicos Tlucco's raid night is on Mondays, and each of the dates correlates to the past fourteen Mondays."

"What's the significance?" Angie queried.

"There are fourteen raid bosses in *Warlords*," Theo explained. "And fourteen seats on the High Council of the Archmagi."

Angie gave him a pained look. "What's the significance for those of us who *aren't* experts on *Warlords*?"

DJ answered for him. "Whatever crazy thing they're trying to do, they've completed all the raids they mean to. They think that they've checked all the boxes before making their next move."

Zahra put her elbows on the desk in front of her, cupping her chin in her hands. "So what's *our* next move?"

"Hang on, Z," Angie said, using Zahra's new nickname among the Magic Club crew. She turned to Tamba and Tayo. "Did you figure out when the next full moon is? And any updates about the sports field?"

Tamba answered her question first. "Next Wednesday night," she said.

"And nothing new about the sports field," Tayo reported. "It's still under construction. The grass is still there, but it's all brown because they haven't been watering it."

The group turned to Angie, waiting for her to put a plan together. She had been the leader of the group since long before Zahra and DJ had joined them, and they all deferred to her.

"Theo and DJ," she said finally, "See what else you can find out about Yteicos Tlucco in *Warlords*. Tayo, Tamba, go with Bridget on Monday to the next Occult Society meeting and pretend you've never heard of them. Find out what they're up to."

Each of the group nodded in turn as they received their assignments. "Z," Angie continued, "play some *Warlords* with DJ this weekend. See if it stirs anything in those dreams of yours."

Zahra felt her lip curl, not excited about playing a video game, even with her best friend. "OK," she conceded reluctantly.

"Alright," Angie said, taking in the whole group with her gaze. "Let's do this."

*****

Zahra's first midterm was the following day, on Friday, in her strongest subject, AP Spanish. Even though the test was administered during her regular class period, the mood in the room felt different than usual. The anticipation in the classroom was palpable, each student simultaneously releasing her or his pent-up anxiety about the onset of the week of midterms, and eagerly anticipating the winter break that tantalized them from beyond.

It felt like a strong start, and Zahra was confident that she had answered the multiple-choice questions to the best of her ability. The essay questions had seemed a bit too easy to Zahra, which made her feel great and nervous at the same time, but she tried to put any worries about the result out of her mind until after the winter break and focus on the tasks at hand.

She spent the weekend studying with DJ and

the Magic Club, who hadn't managed to glean any more information about the Occult Society beyond multiple confirmations that the strange group were indeed planning something big, and that it would happen the next week. Dutifully, Zahra spent some time behind DJ's gaming laptop, feeling ridiculous with his oversized headphones clamped down around her *hijab* and the complex-looking, backlit keyboard and mouse in front of her. DJ had graciously set up the laptop in *Ground Rules* and even created a new *Warlords* character for her — a Djinnborn Fire Mage named "Z" — and showed her the basic controls of the game before putting her in charge.

It took some time getting a hold of the gameplay, but Zahra was able to complete a few quests, fighting some monsters and talking to some of the game's characters to learn more about the story. DJ hovered at her shoulder, giving her pointers and explaining some of the nuances of the game as she played, excited to share something he cared about with his best friend. Zahra found it a little ironic that this was the first time they had actually played a video game together, given how good of friends they had become since meeting in their first week at *GMHS*. They had been assigned to each other as science partners on their first day of classes, and immediately connected over feeling out of place as minorities in the predominantly Caucasian American high school. Truth be told, he was not only her best friend – he was also her only male friend who wasn't South Asian. She felt a tiny bit of self-reproach that it had taken so long for her to exhibit even the smallest semblance of interest in video games, which represented such a strong part of his identity.

After defeating a group of imp-looking creatures and completing another quest, Zahra tugged the headphones off of her ears, grateful for the reprieve. "So, what's the point?"

"What point?" DJ asked.

Zahra pointed at the screen. "I just beat up a bunch of monsters, and finished a quest. And that's after beating up a bunch of other monsters, and finishing another quest. What's the point?"

DJ looked offended. "What's the point of *anything*?" he said testily. "You do quests so your character gains experience, so you can gain more skills and fight bigger, stronger monsters. When your character's strong enough, you can take them into dungeons with other people, or join a guild and fight raid bosses."

"I see," Zahra said dubiously.

"Listen, if you don't like it, you don't have to play it." DJ reached over Zahra to log out of the game, taking the headphones from her. She had undoubtedly hit a nerve.

"No, DJ, I'm sorry," she said, upset that she had hurt his feelings. "I just...don't play any video games, so I'm not sure I understand the bigger picture."

He paused, waiting for her to continue. She could tell from the fire in his eyes that he was angry.

"Let me play some more and see how it goes?" she asked, hoping her continued interest would ameliorate the situation.

DJ looked at her for another moment, then nodded wordlessly. He logged her back into the game, then stepped back and crossed his arms.

Zahra grinned sheepishly, taking the headphones from him. Her Djinnborn Fire Mage looked back at her from within the laptop, waiting for her next move.

*****

Zahra's next exams were European Art History and American Literature on Monday and Tuesday, respectively. Although she felt that she did well on both of them because of her extensive preparation, she spent more time thinking about her visions and everything she and the Magic Club had learned, champing at the bit to hear what Tamba, Tayo, and Bridget had found at the Occult Society meeting on Monday.

Her dreams continued, as intense as ever, but Zahra had learned to roll with the nightly dreamscapes like a bull rider. She found that with great focus, she could zoom in and out of the visions while they were in motion, like she had been able to under Angie's hypnosis, although she couldn't seem to pause them in the same way. The dreams had become a part of her, and always woke her up with a clarion call ringing throughout her consciousness, but no longer drained her of energy or made her feel out of sorts. If anything, they had begun to hone her will to uncover whatever it was that the Occult Society was planning, and defeat it, knowing that her jinn companion, along with DJ and the Magic Club, was in her corner.

To everyone's great disappointment, the two twins and the sleight-of-hand specialist had nothing new to report in their Tuesday meeting about the Occult Society, saying that there was no sign of the group at Davis Library during their regular Monday time slot.

"No blacklight?" Zahra asked, dismayed. "No diagram on the dry erase board? Nothing?"

Tamba and Tayo shook their heads. "Nothing at all," Tamba said. "It looked like no one had used that study room for a while."

"It was strange," Bridget added.

"Very strange," Angie agreed.

*****

With no other information, and time running out quickly, the group had unanimously decided to investigate their suspicions together the following day, on the evening of the full moon.

"Dress comfortably, and be prepared," Angie had said to them ominously.

"Prepared for what?" Theo asked honestly.

"For whatever," Angie retorted irritably. "Who knows what the Occult Society has in store for us."

Zahra received a reprieve from classes on Wednesday afternoon, having completed her Biology exam in the morning and only requested to turn in a portfolio for Advanced Photography. PhysEd didn't require any sort of test, which meant that her Algebra II midterm, on Thursday, would be her last of the semester.

She spent the afternoon reviewing problem sets on her own, preferring the noisy atmosphere of *Ground Rules* to the quietude of Davis Library, which she now associated with the Occult Society and wanted to avoid in any case. DJ joined her as afternoon turned into evening, after his own midterm in another class and the final swim practice of the season.

He entered the cafe wearing the strangest outfit Zahra had seen him in, even considering that they'd spent their fair share of Halloweens together. A long, flowing velvet cloak had been tied around his neck, and he had belted a blue tunic over what looked like cargo pants. A six-foot walking staff was gripped in his right hand, clicking against the cafe floor as he approached her.

"What?" she asked, taking in his appearance.

DJ looked down at his outfit. "What?" he countered. "Angie said to be prepared."

Zahra kept her expression neutral, realizing

that DJ was taking the *Warlords of Gunthor* aspect of their evening activity very seriously. She thought about her own outfit of jeans, a sweatshirt, and a simple headscarf, and the kind of looks they would receive from passersby on the short walk to *GMHS*.

She was grateful that it was already dark out.

As had been previously agreed upon, Zahra and DJ met the Magic Club at their school's rear entrance, an expansive parking lot that overlooked the sports field and the campus proper. They trotted up to the rest of the group, who were already waiting in the shadows of the empty lot under a full, orange moon overhead.

Angie and Bridget were both dressed casually in jeans and hoodies, the latter's crutches glinting silvery in the moonlight. Tayo and Tamba wore matching warmups and *GMHS* soccer jackets, and Tayo held a soccer ball in the crook of his arm. Theo was dressed almost exactly the same as DJ, although Zahra couldn't make out the colors of his outfit in the dim light, and instead of a walking staff, he held a styrofoam shield with the *Warlords of Gunthor* logo painted on it.

They were a motley crew, but Zahra was grateful for them.

"Alright," Angie said as Zahra and DJ joined them. DJ and Theo looked each other up and down once, noting their matching outfits, and nodded their approval.

"What's the plan?" Zahra asked.

"Tayo scouted ahead," Tamba explained. "It looks like the Occult Society is there already, doing something."

"I couldn't see what they were up to from the edge of the parking lot," Tayo said. "But they're definitely there."

Zahra shivered in the cold night air. Winter was definitely on its way. "What should we do?"

"We came here to figure out what they're up to, and to stop it," Angie said confidently. "So that's what we'll do."

The others didn't seem to share her conviction. "What if they...I don't know...start a fight or something?" Tamba asked.

"Then we're ready," Theo said, brandishing his shield ridiculously.

Even in the moonlight, Zahra could see Angie roll her eyes. "We'll handle it," she said simply.

The little group walked together to the edge of the parking lot and onto a small service road that coiled several hundreds of feet below to the school grounds. A handful of construction vehicles were parked on the shoulder of the road, and stout oak and sycamore trees ringed the field, blocking the majority of it from view. As they neared the perimeter of the sports field, Zahra thought she could see flashing lights emanating from its center.

Zahra followed DJ and the Magic Club through several lazy switchbacks down onto a long asphalt corridor that ran the length of the sports field and eventually to the school proper, to meet with a small intra-campus road and the gymnasium. The field opened to her right, a hundred yards or more of pitch that had been allowed to devolve into brittle, yellow grass while the area was closed for renovations. Extensive lengths of aluminum bleachers sat in various states of construction on either side of the field, and several soccer goals stood forgotten in one corner, pressed against one another as though huddling together away from the cold.

At the center of the grassy field, Zahra could make out several shadows moving back and forth, flashlights casting erratic bursts of light that provided splashes of focused color which the orange moon overhead couldn't hope to reproduce. Among the shadows were several patches of deeper darkness, standing out against the pitch in stark relief.

At the head of their group, Angie looked back once, her white eyes gleaming in the dimness, then stepped over a strip of yellow construction tape and onto the sports field. The rest of the Magic Club followed dutifully, while DJ and Zahra brought up the rear.

The moment Zahra's foot touched the field, something changed. Her senses immediately felt heightened, and a prickly feeling crawled up her spine to rest behind her ears. A frigid breeze whipped across the open space, but the cold couldn't touch her, and she felt a comfortable warmth spread throughout her extremities. The dry grass under her feet crunched loudly in her ears, and she could hear her friends breathing, warm gusts of air mixing with the wind to create a vortex of sound.

Ahead, the lights continued to flash, and Zahra could clearly make out five shadows encircling some type of apparatus with flashlights and what looked like newly burning torches in their hands. Each of the shadows moved as one to bend towards smaller structures that surrounded the apparatus, lighting them in turn with the torches that burned orange and red in the dark.

Zahra wasn't sure if time began to speed up, or slow down. Her body moved of its own volition, following the Magic Club instinctively as they all saw the fires being lit in a circle around the central apparatus. The group broke into a run, saying nothing, knowing that irrespective of whatever ritual was being performed, the dry pitch underfoot would be like kindling.

The wind whipped past Zahra's headscarf, unnoticed as she focused on the circle of fire that awaited ahead. The cold air bit at her throat and nostrils, unheeded, and her body warmed with the physical exertion and a feeling of certainty that she had been unconsciously craving for the past month. Her vision swam with the glare of the fires as they met the orange light of the moon and cast the field in a crimson radiance that was familiar and alien at the same time. She ran with purpose, feeling a blaze stoking within her that matched the brilliance of the conflagration in front of her, acting on instinct and observing her surroundings as though from a very great distance.

"Call the police!" she heard Angie call back to Bridget, who was struggling to keep up with the group on her crutches.

As they neared the inferno, Zahra saw the members of the Occult Society, dressed in their matching glow-in-the-dark Gunthor t-shirts, exposed to the cold night air with torches extended in front of them. A pentagram of fire surrounded them, knee-high three-dimensional mandalas that represented the *Warlords* raid symbols, constructed from some sort of dark wood that burned brightly in the dry breeze. The students themselves surrounded a wicker oval, stretching their arms to ignite it as one.

It was the spitting image of the portal from Zahra's dream and *Warlords of Gunthor*. Rudimentary wooden claws gripped the oval on the top and bottom, and the whole thing had to be at least six feet tall. Kindling had been strewn below the portal, undoubtedly to help prop up the huge oval and ensure that it burned.

There was no question in Zahra's mind that if the Occult Society managed to ignite the portal, the entire field would catch fire in no time. It wouldn't take long for the conflagration to reach the gymnasium, and perhaps the school beyond.

Everything happened at once, without much discussion between the Magic Club members. Tayo was the first to react, his athlete's reflexes lending him the speed and agility to move quickly, and he tossed the soccer ball in front of him, kicking it with such force before it hit the ground that it sped like an arrow towards the oblong portal. His aim wasn't as good as his power, however, and the missile missed its mark, veering wildly in the night air. It still managed to strike one of the Occult Society students, a shadow who was only recognizable to Zahra by his camouflage hat that looked red and black in the firelight, knocking the torch from his hands.

Tamba and Angie ran straight for the pentagon of burning symbols, stripping off their jackets and slapping them against the wooden constructions and trying to prevent the fires from spreading. DJ charged into the circle of students, his voice rising like a battle cry over the din of the fire and wind, his cloak trailing behind him and the walking stick brandished horizontally in front of him clumsily like a shopping cart. Theo huffed behind him, not as athletic but no less enthusiastic, bowling into the nearest Occult Society members with his protective shield. The pair wrestled awkwardly with the two platinum blonde boys and the red-haired girl, while Tayo, who had caught up, crashed into the student he had hit with the soccer ball.

The Occult Society leader, positioned on a small stepstool in the middle of the carnage, paid no heed to the commotion around him. He stood on his tiptoes, attempting to ignite the portal in between the two claws at the apex of the oval.

The world dropped away from Zahra, and she felt another force take hold of her body as she stood just outside the pentagram. The full moon overhead mingled with the heat from the fires in front of her, drowning the field in shades of vermillion and scarlet, and the intermingled students capered like shadows spilling from the central portal, haze and smoke roiling within. Zahra's arm extended of its own accord, pointing towards the Occult Society leader with undeniable purpose, her eyes mired with the flame-filled reflection of the inferno.

"*STOP*," she commanded, her voice heavy with power.

The group of students, her friends as well as the Occult Society, froze in place to regard her. Angie and Tamba looked at her from the edge of the pentagram, their mouths dropping from the sound that emerged from their normally understated friend. DJ, Theo, Tayo, and their opponents likewise paused in their melee, peering through the smoke in astonishment. The Occult Society leader's head snapped towards her, a mixture of anger, surprise, and fear playing across his features.

What they saw in her expression, Zahra

couldn't say. She felt the heat of the fire play along her outstretched arm and dance across her body, the jade prayer beads encircling her wrist shining incandescently in the night. Flames smoldered around the corners of her eyes and the breeze whipped her headscarf around her face. The orange moonlight made her look otherworldly, a supernatural being cradled in fire in defiance of the frigid wind.

"Stop," she ordered again, more quietly, but with no less conviction.

The Occult Society leader's face shifted, anger and determination winning out over reason, and he began to turn back towards the portal, his torch ready to light it on fire.

Slicing through the darkness, tearing through the smoke, wind and haze, whistled a lone playing card. It struck the leader in one of his shark-black eyes, causing him to drop the torch at his feet and claw at his face with both hands. He stumbled off his perch with a yelp, and Tayo jumped onto his torch, stamping it out with his foot.

"Got him," Bridget breathed, leaning heavily on her crutches just outside the pentagon.

In the distance, a fire engine siren pealed, its clarion call renting the night.

Epilogue

Zahra could not have been happier with the way her Algebra II midterm turned out. She wasn't sure if Mr. Ryan had intentionally made the test easy compared to the practice problems, but she found the answers flowing through her onto the page. She snuck a grin now and then at DJ, who sat across from her at their little work table, the fresh scratch marks on his face from the night before giving him a hardcore, if still handsome, look about him.

The Magic Club met for the last Thursday of the semester, sharing their lunch together and processing the events of the previous evening. Zahra and her friends had been able to prevent the blaze from spreading too widely, stamping out the torches and constructions to the best of their ability until the fire department arrived moments later. A couple of the would-be arsonists had escaped, but were easily identified by their association with the Occult Society, and were all suspended from school while an investigation was opened. Zahra's friends had survived the experience relatively unscathed, and were treated by the authorities for minor burns and bruises.

"You were awesome, Z," Theo said in their meeting, his voice whistling through a new gap in his teeth.

"Thanks," Zahra said, blushing. "You too."

When pressed, no one was able to tell her what it was about her appearance the previous night that had stunned them, or why she had been able to halt the brawl with a single word. Zahra's friends said that she just looked confident, and were a little scared of her, particularly because she was usually so quiet.

Through some research on the part of Theo and DJ's respective guilds, they were able to confirm that members among Yteicos Tlucco in *Warlords of Gunthor* had begun to scatter, not wanting to be associated with what was being called "attempted arson and destruction of school property." Zahra's group had thrown a wrench in a semester-long, cultish plan to release the minions of Arturia onto Earth, or some similar nonsense that the Occult Society members had concocted. One person in Theo's guild had told him that the Occult Society leader, whom they learned wasn't even a *GMHS* student, had read a book about portals somewhere and had pressed his ideas among the group through sending messages in Yteicos Tlucco. The Magic Club agreed that the cult's motives didn't really matter, and that Zahra's visions ultimately turned out to be the only defense against their machinations.

"Your dreams were right," Angie said simply, and they decided to leave it at that.

Emboldened by their experience, DJ wore his *Warlords of Gunthor* sweatshirt proudly, begging Zahra to play the game with him again that weekend in the hopes that their adventures had sparked a new interest in it for her. She agreed reluctantly, more to have something to look forward to as they started winter break than from any real desire to kill more monsters.

She hadn't seen Vazir, except in passing around school, since the Winter Formal, and had tried to avoid him out of embarrassment as much as possible. To her surprise, he texted her after school was over on Thursday, wishing her a nice winter break and asking if she'd like to join him, with her parents and brother, at a winter solstice party being thrown by his family. It was an easy, neutral, and importantly, parent-approved way for them to spend some time together.

I'd like that, she responded to his text. The idea of hanging out with him, around their families, warmed her heart.

That night, Zahra deliberately spent time watching TV with her family, feeling the stress of her midterms and the semester melting away behind her. Thoughts of the past month came and went, images of the icy-themed Winter Formal clashing with fire-swept fields and falling away to nothingness. A pair of crimson-rimmed eyes peeked out at the edge of her vision, the wind outside of her family's house carrying soot-laced whispers that only she could hear. Every once in a while, a mirage of the sports field would flash across her eyes like lightning, and she would see herself pointing ominously at the yawning portal, wreathed in fire and surging with power. As the night went on, the apparitions became fewer and farther between, and Zahra slowly settled into her spot on the floor opposite her brother, easing bit by bit back into the world around her.

She yawned happily, tired but knowing that she would sleep well. She mused, with a little sadness and a tremendous amount of relief, about how her dreams had left her the night before, disappearing into a void of blissful slumber after the skirmish on the crimson field. She couldn't remember having slept better, and looked forward to greeting her bed again. A tiny piece of her wondered about the flamewalker from her visions, and whether she would see it again. After dreaming about it every night for a month, she had become accustomed to its familiar presence, and felt remorse for her initial suspicions about her fiery companion. She pondered on whether it would appear to her again, or if the dreamscapes would continue to dissolve altogether now that the danger had passed. Time would tell, she supposed.

"What are you thinking about, *beta*?" her mother asked from the couch, rolling up her sleeves to peel an orange for Zahra's brother, who sat at her mother's feet, chewing on a scoured popsicle stick.

Zahra shook her head, realizing she had been daydreaming. "Nothing, mummy," she said. "Just happy to be done with school."

"Happy to be done with your maths test," her father said proudly from his chair.

Zahra couldn't agree more.

ABOUT THE AUTHOR

M. S. Farzan was born in London, UK and grew up
in the San Francisco Bay Area. He has a Ph.D. in
Cultural and Historical Studies of Religions, and has
written and worked for high-profile video game
companies and editorial websites such as Electronic
Arts, Perfect World Entertainment, and
MMORPG.com. He also enjoys soccer, baseball,
martial arts, and games of all kinds.